THE PERFECT BLEND

A.D. ELLIS

Michael & Tenise,
Thank you for your help with the song and the title.

ONE

JUSTIN WADE

"WELCOME TO PIPING HOT," the middle-aged woman behind the counter called out as the bells tinkled to announce my arrival.

The coffee shop was nearly empty, but for a weekday mid-afternoon in a small town like Briarton, that wasn't unusual. Earlier that morning, the shop would have been filled with locals grabbing coffee and breakfast before heading to work—many in the neighboring city—and several of the retired folks gathered around sipping their drinks well into mid-morning.

With my plans for the place, I envisioned a steady stream of business and a full-house throughout the day. Who wouldn't want to spend their time in a comfy cozy coffee shop sipping a delicious brew, munching on delightful baked goods, and meeting with folks over a board game, a book, or a hobby?

I gave a quick wave to the friendly woman behind the counter. I wondered briefly if she'd want to stay on when I took over. With the money and unwavering support from my grandpa, a dream, and a whole lot of gumption guiding my way, I headed toward the man at the far corner table.

My meeting with Joe, the building owner—Piping Hot was housed in a perfect corner location of a larger building—technically wasn't for another five minutes, but early was on time in my book and I was anxious to make a good first impression.

The man appeared to be nearing fifty with salt-n-pepper hair and a smooth, angular jawline I guessed would be showing scruff by dinnertime. It was hard to judge his height, but I estimated he was possibly just a bit taller than my five foot nine inches. He was broader in the chest and shoulders than me, but we both appeared to be of average build. I caught a quick glimpse of intense green eyes as he glanced up at my approach. The man was gorgeous, but I pushed away the fleeting attraction—I was here to impress him and buy Piping Hot, not drool over a silver fox.

"Hi," I said, hoping I sounded both friendly and professional, "I'm Justin Wade. Thank you for taking time to meet with me. I look forward to sharing my plans for purchasing Piping Hot."

The man's eyebrow arched slightly, but he took my outstretched hand.

His lack of words set me on edge, but I'd known from the few emails we'd exchanged, and what my grandpa cryptically told me about Joe, he was a bit eccentric.

Determined to never again be steamrolled and taken advantage of in a business deal, I took his silence as a challenge and pulled out a chair. "As I explained in our emails, I have a solid plan to take Piping Hot from what it is now to something grand."

"Justin Wade you say? How did you come to be in Briarton, Mr. Wade?" The man cocked his head and studied me with a bemused look.

Only slightly thrown off my game—did he not remember we'd corresponded more than once and my grandfather was a lifelong resident of the little town?—I switched gears momentarily. "My grandfather, Harley Wade, has lived here his entire life." My nerves calmed slightly when recognition crossed Joe's face. "My father jetted the moment he turned eighteen, but I'd visit Grandpa every summer while the rest of my family traveled and schmoozed. I've recently opted to leave the big city life—it wasn't for me—and live here with Harley." Attempting to move the conversation back to the reason I was there, I forged on. "With my business management degree and exemplary baking skills, not to mention my interest in both coffee and tea, I know I can take Piping Hot to the next level."

I wasn't about to mention my last huge business idea had been an epic failure. Honestly, the idea was great, the person I trusted to help me make it happen had turned out to be an absolute jerk. Sean, my ex, had greedily accepted my entire savings to get our start-up off the ground.

And then he'd ghosted me.

My boyfriend of nearly two years.

My lifelong savings.

My big idea.

All gone in the blink of an eye.

Sean, when I finally cornered him, after waiting at his apartment for three hours, swore it was just how business worked with start-ups. Said it was a risk and we'd failed. I knew better, but there was nothing I could do. We'd had no contracts or official business accounts at the time. I'd readily handed over the money thinking he'd use it for all the start-up costs—he'd convinced me *I* was the big idea man and he was the details guy—and then he'd bounced.

After berating myself severely and licking my wounds for a month—and quickly realizing, no matter how hard I tried to be a big city guy, the city just wasn't for me—I'd called Harley and poured out my whole pathetic story. He'd offered me the guest house on his property and, at twenty-eight years of age, I'd moved to Briarton a week later.

With no plans for exactly what I'd do for employment once I got to town, I'd been floored when Grandpa, a retired pediatrician, sat me down and explained he'd put aside a large chunk of money for whichever grandchild ever decided to take the small-town route. He'd handed over a large sum of money, told me to spend it wisely, and handed me a flyer advertising the sale of Piping Hot.

Within seconds, my dream of owning a business *and* putting my baking skills to good use had been a potential reality.

I just had to convince the guy across the table from me I was the perfect person to buy the coffee shop in his building.

He cleared his throat and pursed his lips. "And what, in your opinion, needs to be done to take the place to the next level?"

Fighting the urge to rub my hands together and really dive in, I smiled. "Well, the best thing the place has going for it is the atmosphere. Already smells great, gives off a very comfortable, cozy, welcoming vibe, and has an amazing aesthetic with the exposed brick and mixture of wooden beams and black iron."

He glanced around and nodded. "It really is a great little shop."

I pounced. "But it could be so much better."

The guy raised a brow. "Go on."

Inwardly fist pumping because I had him on the hook, I opened my folder. I didn't *need* the information inside, but I knew it looked very polished and professional to have paperwork regarding plans for a business.

"I'm not only a business management major, I'm also a baker. I'll increase the variety and quality of the baked goods by ten-fold and have customers watering at the mouth for their favorites." I pulled out a list of the improvements I planned to make and closed the folder. "I'll also increase the quality of coffees and teas we serve. After a quick perusal of the website—which I'll also overhaul—I noticed our coffee beans are mediocre and our tea is fairly blah. I want to level up on both the type and variety of coffee and tea we offer." I purposely launched into speaking in a way that already claimed the shop as mine.

"Sounds like you plan to change a lot," Joe mused.

Picking up on the fact he may not like all the talk of *change*, I shook my head. "Not so much *change*, just increase our appeal. More and better baked goods, breakfast sandwiches, coffees, and teas. Plus, a bit down the road, simple soups and sandwiches to bring the morning crowd back for lunch."

He once again looked intrigued.

"And, the part I'm maybe the most excited about, I want to use the space to offer folks a place to set up games, have book clubs, do scrapbooking, yarn crafts, and such."

"So, you feel the current state of Piping Hot is far from where it *could* be?" he asked.

"I do, I really do. It's a great little place, don't get me wrong. But it could be so much more." I kept the tremor out of my voice and didn't let myself think about what happened if he didn't let me buy this coffee shop.

"And you're the person to do it? Take it to the next level?" Those brilliant green eyes locked on mine in challenge and I once again had to push aside the thought of how damn gorgeous he was.

"I am." My confidence wasn't bravado. I'd been screwed over by Sean, but that was because I'd been stupid enough to go into business with a lover. I was sure of my plans and my ability to grow Piping Hot into something Briarton never knew it was missing.

"And why would you be a better person for the job than any of the other prospective buyers?"

Easy.

"I'm young, I'm passionate, and I have a solid plan. In addition, I'm a talented baker and I have a fairly wide base knowledge of coffees and teas. Plus, I'm a local."

He frowned. "Local? You just moved here."

I shrugged. "But I've been here most of my life during the summers and I have family here. Can the other potential buyers say that? Doubt it. They probably want to buy it and send someone else to manage it without ever even stepping foot in the place. I'm interested in more than just an investment. This place will be my baby and the pride and joy of the entire town."

The chimes over the door announced an arrival and I glanced toward the front of the shop.

Shaken slightly, my eyes widened a bit to see Grandpa with a tall, willowy woman. She wore a flowy shirt which cascaded over her slim hips into a gauzy skirt, several mismatched pieces of jewelry, and a pair of Birkenstocks on her bare feet. Her silver hair was styled in an artfully messy bob and a pair of cat-eye glasses perched on her nose.

"Ah, good, you're already here," Grandpa said.

The man across the table from me stood and shook hands with both new arrivals. "Harley, Jo Ellen, it's nice to see you both."

Grandpa turned to me and smiled broadly. "Justin, I wanted to introduce you before your meeting got started." He gestured toward the woman. "This is my girlfriend, Jo."

I caught myself before the confused frown could take over my face, stuck out my hand with a polite smile, and said hello. "Nice to meet you. I didn't know Grandpa was dating." I shot a look at Harley and he blushed. My grandpa actually blushed.

As I glanced around the little group of four, something wasn't adding up but I couldn't quite put my finger on it.

"Well, um, maybe we could catch up a bit later? I'd like to continue our meeting." I hated to rush them off, but I *needed* this meeting to go well. I could almost taste Piping Hot being mine.

"Of course, of course," Harley said. "I'll leave you to it."

"Stay, dear. I've never seen the sense in starched, boring meetings. Let's just get some drinks and have ourselves a conversation." Jo Ellen motioned toward the table.

The man I'd been speaking to quickly made room for the four of us to sit down and Grandpa went to the counter for drinks.

"Now," Jo Ellen peered over her glasses at me, "I know of Morgan's interest in buying Piping Hot. But tell me, Justin Wade, what exactly is *your* reason for wanting to purchase in my building?"

A quick look toward the silver fox I'd spent ten minutes blathering on to showed a smug smirk on his face.

Wait.

What in the hell was going on?

Jo Ellen was the building owner?

And she was dating my grandpa?

Suddenly a few things slipped into place.

Harley had mentioned *Joe* as the owner and I'd been emailing with the owner—had I missed the name being *Jo* rather than *Joe*? All this time I'd ridiculously assumed the building owner was a man.

Nope.

A woman.

A very eccentric, odd, and opinionated woman.

Who was dating my grandpa.

Then who the hell had I just spilled my business plan to?

TWO

MORGAN PERRY

JUST WHO IN the hell did this kid think he was?

Gorgeous, sexy, and adorably pumped up with his big plans, but still, just who the hell did he think he was?

Waltzed right in and started telling *me* all the ways Piping Hot could be better once *he* was the owner.

What the hell ever.

I wanted Piping Hot.

I *needed* Piping Hot.

Granted, I'd only been in Briarton just a bit over six months, and there was still *a lot* I wanted to do with the little coffee shop once *I* owned it. But I'd already made improvements as the manager and I had a lot more in the works.

In truth, some of Justin's plans sounded really great, but it wasn't like I wouldn't have been able to come up with most of those on my own. Okay, I wasn't a baker so he had me on that point, but the rest was definitely doable.

After my husband had died of a massive heart attack a couple years earlier, I'd doubled down in my high-stress corporate finance job, determined to work away the devastating loss of my best friend. If I was so busy I couldn't breathe, then there was no way I'd feel the pain. Until the stress got to be too much and my doctor declared I had to stop working or I'd be following James to an early grave.

While I'd definitely *felt* emotionally and physically dead after years and years in that job, I didn't *want* to die. James never would have wanted me working myself to death. So, I'd quit my job, packed up my empty apartment, and threw a dart at a map.

Okay, in reality, I'd closed my eyes and pointed to a map —I didn't have darts just lying around my house—but the idea was the same. My finger landed on Briarton, smackdab in the middle of the Midwest. I kept most of my money in my New York bank accounts—everything could be done online these days—withdrew enough cash to open new accounts in my new location, donated most of my belongings to charity, and traded in my sleek BMW for a Jeep more suitable for where I was going.

I said goodbye to New York and never looked back.

The little town of Briarton had accepted the big city transplant with open arms and I'd quickly fallen in love with Piping Hot after taking a job there as a way to get to know the locals. Money was something I had plenty of and I'd decided right away if the little coffee shop ever went up for sale, I'd snatch it up.

Not only would owning Piping Hot be a solid investment, it would be something I could pour my heart and soul into. Losing James had been rough and I'd forever miss him, but his absence brought to light I had very little I was passionate about. I was good at a lot of things. James and I had had a solid, comfortable relationship. But I hadn't felt the spark of passion and excitement about something in...well, in most of my adult life.

Piping Hot was going to change that for me. I already felt

a connection to the place and I wanted to devote time and energy into making it the best little coffee shop in the Midwest.

Jo Ellen Lucas, the owner of the entire building, had slowly been renting out the businesses and spaces within. She'd stated she'd own the actual building until the day she died, but she planned to rent or sell many of the businesses housed in the building.

And I wanted Piping Hot.

Apparently, so did Justin Wade.

The very young, very attractive grandson of Harley Wade.

Harley and Jo were about as mismatched as a couple could be, but something definitely kept them coming back to each other. They'd not been dating long, but the flirting had been obvious even back when I came to town.

How was I going to compete with the eager young business major and baker when he had such a great plan and his grandpa was dating the seller?

Smirking at his confusion—I'd known the moment he started his pitch he mistakenly thought I was the owner—and wondered if he'd recover.

Who was I kidding? The kid seemed invincible. Of course, he'd recover.

And he did.

But not before I saw the flustered flush on his cheeks from the quick wink I gave him. He teetered and tottered, but quickly regained his footing.

"Well, as I was telling *Morgan*, I have some great plans for Piping Hot. As I'm sure Harley has told you, I'm a very talented baker." Justin launched into his business plan as if his speech to me had just been his warm-up.

By the end, Jo Ellen was beaming. "Well, those sound like fabulous ideas, dear."

Harley patted Justin's arm.

"Morgan, I know you'd been toying with many of the same changes and upgrades," Jo said. "I'm in quite the predicament. You both seem like you'd be the perfect owners and I know Piping Hot would be in great hands with either of you." She sipped her coffee and eyed us over the mug. "My issue comes down to family."

My heart sank. There it was. The kid was going to swoop in and take what I wanted simply because he was Harley's grandson.

I adored the older man and I was getting used to Jo Ellen's quirks. But damned if it didn't sting to have my hopes dashed.

"If you boys have done any kind of research on the other businesses in my building," Jo continued, "you already know I've made it my mission to ensure a *family-owned* theme within my building. If I can't assure a downhome, stable, loving, welcoming feel with family-owned businesses, I won't be selling off sections within my building. It's as simple as that."

Justin tossed a smug look my way. "Nothing more family-oriented than the grandson of the town's beloved pediatrician owning the comfy cozy coffee shop."

Jo chuckled. "Well, yes, but *family-owned by association* isn't exactly the feel I'm looking for." She pursed her lips and studied me. "Morgan, you've become a truly valued member of this town…" she trailed off.

"Jo, dear, if the men can assure a family-owned *feel*, perhaps an exception could be made?" Harley suggested.

"Nonsense," Jo said as she patted Harley's hand. "I'm not in *need* of selling parcels within my building. If Piping Hot is to be bought, it will be bought by family, run by family, and presented as family. If not, it won't be sold."

I knew enough about Jo Ellen's opinionated oddities to understand she wouldn't be budging from her stance on this.

Harley frowned—clearly knowing his girlfriend well enough to know she was set on the issue—and glanced between Justin and me. "Well, boys, unless you're secretly planning to tie the knot and co-own a coffee shop, I think you're out of luck."

I could see the sorrow in the older man's eyes. He'd been so excited about Justin moving to Briarton. If the kid didn't get the coffee shop, would he leave town?

As if my life had turned into a slow-motion gag reel, I realized with a shock Justin had reached for my hand. When my brain finally registered the warmth of his strong hand holding mine, I dragged my eyes to his determined face and tried to comprehend his words.

"My apologies, Ms. Lucas," he started.

"Nonsense, call me Jo."

"Jo," Justin amended. "I've been in the city too long and private family life was never expected to be a part of business. Seeing as how I'm adjusting to my new life in Briarton, I'll have to learn my private family life is valued here."

He brought my hand to his lips and brushed a kiss over the knuckles—soft, pink lips sending warmth through me. What in the hell was happening?

Harley cleared his throat, evidently as confused as I was. "Justin, son?"

"Grandpa, Jo, I wasn't planning on telling you this way, but Morgan and I are engaged."

THREE
JUSTIN

MORGAN'S entire body tensed and his hand gripped mine while Grandpa sputtered and Jo Ellen eyed our joined hands, a twinkle of joy dancing just behind a layer of suspicion.

I'd been forced into an *act now, ask for forgiveness later* situation and I prayed it would pay off.

Giving Morgan what I hoped to be a convincing *we'll figure this out* smile, I squeezed his hand. "Sorry, I know we were wanting to keep it to ourselves for a little longer, but I know how badly we both want to see Piping Hot become the best it can be."

Jo shook off her initial suspicions and clapped her hands with a giddy squeal. "Har-ley," she drawled, "you didn't tell me!"

Grandpa gaped like a dying fish. "I didn't know. How… when…I don't…" his garbled words trailed off as I saw him attempting to figure out what had just happened.

Grandpa would have to believe the farce. He was obviously too smitten with Jo Ellen and I wasn't going to risk him telling her I'd just made up being involved with Morgan.

If the plan was going to work, everyone had to believe it.

As far as details regarding specifics of our fake engagement, we'd deal with those later. Once we owned Piping Hot, Morgan and I could work something out. I'd buy him out, let him stay on as manager, whatever.

"Oh, this changes everything," Jo gushed. "When is the wedding?"

The grip on my hand was a vice and I barely avoided wincing. "We haven't set anything in stone. We've been so busy with plans for Piping Hot. When we finally get around to it, it will be something simple. Very quick and small. Morgan and I aren't the type to want anything extravagant."

"Nonsense, none of this *getting around to it* garbage," Jo said. "I'll work on getting purchase papers drawn up, but the deal won't be finalized until you're officially married." She beamed. "Piping Hot is one of my favorite businesses in this building. Knowing it will be under the good care of a loving couple such as yourselves is just the happy news I needed today."

Grandpa took Jo's hand. "Should we give them some time to discuss their plans?"

"Yes, of course." Jo stood. "You boys will let us know of the date? Perhaps we could be your witnesses? Once it's all said and done, we'll work on the other details."

I think I nodded, but the reality of the situation was sinking in and I may have been in shock.

"Justin," Grandpa's sharp voice pulled me back to the surface, "I'll see you at home." It wasn't a question or a request, it was a demand.

"I'll be there in a bit," I said.

When they were gone, Morgan yanked his hand from mine and whispered harshly, "What the hell was that? What did you just do?"

I glanced toward the woman behind the counter who was pretending to clean the espresso machine and gave Morgan a quick shake of my head. Grabbing his hand and pulling him to stand, I headed toward where I assumed an office would be.

Darting into the door at the far end of the small hallway, I finally let go of his hand and turned to face an angry Morgan. "I just saved our asses out there."

"By getting us involved in a fake marriage so we can own a coffee shop in Small-Town, USA?" Morgan barked a laugh. "Thanks, but no, thanks."

"Look, you were there. I barely know her, but I could tell there was no changing her mind. She wanted a *family* to own Piping Hot. You heard her, she doesn't *need* to sell. You want this place. I want this place." I shrugged, suddenly wondering if I'd made a huge mistake. "I noticed a rainbow bracelet on her wrist and took a chance she wouldn't mind a gay couple as long as we fit with her family-owned theme."

Morgan ran a hand over his face. "I guess you lucked out I'm gay."

That comment gave me pause. "Sorry, I guess I just assumed. Shit, I didn't like out you or something, did I?"

He sighed wearily. "I'm gay. No, you didn't out me. Harley and Jo have been great friends since I moved here."

"I can't believe I didn't know they were dating." I paced the office floor. "I can't believe I thought *you* were the owner. Why did I not realize Jo was a female?" I pulled out my phone and searched my email. Scanning our latest correspondence I saw where my mistake had been. "Jo's signature is *JoE Lucas*. Didn't really register the odd capitalization, just saw Joe and went with it. That's what assuming things will get me." I huffed.

Morgan gave a little chuckle. "Well, Jo is nothing if not odd." He eyed me for a moment. "So, your first plan was just to tell them we're engaged, buy the place, and then never get around to marrying, right?"

My lips twisted. "Yeah. Too bad Jo trashed that idea."

His brow furrowed. "And the plan now?"

I flopped down at the desk. "How do you feel about a summer wedding?" I deadpanned.

A nervous laugh erupted from Morgan. "Are you for real? You think we should get married just so we can own this place?"

Leaning forward, my elbows on the desk, I steepled my fingers under my chin. "I want this place. I got completely screwed over in a business situation back in the city. Moving to Briarton with my grandpa has given me a second chance. I'm a damned good baker and I know I can make this place amazing."

"So you've said," Morgan replied with a smirk.

My cheeks heated. "How badly do you want this place?"

He crossed his arms over his chest. "I'm guessing only slightly less than you. I left big city corporate finance for my mental and physical health. Ending up in Briarton was simple luck. Piping Hot was supposed to be just my outlet and a way to meet people, but I really like the place and I think it can be something great." He scowled as if a thought hit him. "I think I really *need* the place. Need something to pour my heart into."

I stood and rounded the desk. "Then we're on the same page with that part. There's no way Jo is selling if we're not *family*."

"So, what, we just marry a stranger because it comes with a coffee shop and baked goods?"

Facing him, I shoved my hands in my pocket. "We need to think through details, but I'm thinking we marry, buy the place, give things a bit of time so it's not too obvious—and we'll need time to get Piping Hot set up the way we want it— and then we can quietly dissolve our marriage."

"And what about the business?"

I shrugged. "I can buy you out or we can make it work. You strike me as a smart person with a good work ethic. I'd be grateful to have you as co-owner. We can work through it all when the time comes, but first, we have to get those papers signed and buy the place."

Morgan took a deep breath. "I was married once. Never thought I'd marry again after James died."

His words tugged at my heart. "What you had with James was real." I didn't *know* that, but I assumed he'd had a good marriage if he was talking so fondly about it. "I'd never expect to take that away. This will be a front for our business deal. Nothing more."

His eyes caught mine. "I don't want to make a mockery of marriage. James and I loved each other, but if I'm being completely honest, we weren't the crazy-in-love romantic couple. We were a partnership. If we do this, I don't want it to be a regret or a joke. We go into it as a partnership— whether we know it has an end date or not."

I wondered at his words and his past with James. I'd always thought I'd marry because I was head-over-heels in love, not because it made good business sense as partners. But if marrying Morgan in order to make Piping Hot mine was what had to happen, I'd push aside my preconceived notions of marriage and make it work.

"I think looking at it as a business partnership is a good idea," I said.

"Should we maybe sit down and figure out specifics and such? Maybe private life details first then coffee shop details?" Morgan suddenly seemed tired and possibly overwhelmed.

"Yeah, that's probably a really good idea." I glanced at my phone. "Harley wants to interrogate me, so I better get going. Can we maybe do lunch tomorrow and hash it all out?"

"Are we sure this is a good plan?"

I chuckled. "No. But it's the best we've got if we want to buy this place."

"I do."

"I do, too. So, I guess we're doing this."

Morgan studied me for a bit. "Why do you want it so badly? I mean, you don't have to prove anything to me. I get that the only way either of us is getting this place is if we do it together, but what's your driving force?"

I sighed. "My parents and siblings are all jet-setting travelers, big city people—I've never fit in with them. Over the years, I did my best to make myself one of them. I did college in the city and did my very best to survive urban life, but it wasn't for me. When an ex screwed me over and I lost everything, I had no choice but to tuck tail and turn to Harley." I shrugged. "But more than that, I was ready to leave the hustle and bustle. The city wore me out and brought me down. Briarton? Harley? Small-town living? It's what I've always longed for and I finally stopped pretending I was like the rest of my family." Crossing my arms over my chest, I continued. "I'm a business management major, but big business has never appealed to me. Baking, coffee, tea, bringing people together? Those are simple things I can get excited about. Piping Hot would allow me to be somewhere that makes me happy, be near my grandpa, and be successful. Not to the level my parents would ever consider actual success, but I finally gave up trying to live up to their expectations because I'm just not that person."

Morgan nodded but didn't say anything.

"What about you? Why Piping Hot?"

"James died of a massive heart attack. We worked the same job and I tried to pour myself into my work even more after his death. My mental and physical health suffered. I was slowly killing myself with my job and the fast pace." He got a faraway look in his eyes. "I sold my cold apartment, traded my suits for jeans and flannels, and picked a town. Briarton has breathed new life into me and I finally no longer feel like I'm drowning in grief and burn-out." Shaking his head as if to clear a memory, Morgan went on. "Piping Hot has been my lifeline as I've found a routine, a purpose, and made actual friends. Nothing in my big city life ever made me feel as centered and grounded as a simple job at a coffee shop."

"We both have good reasons and a good plan for the place. Our method of getting this to work is a bit shaky, but I think we can pull it off." I opened a new contact on my phone. "I should probably have my fiancé's number."

Morgan snorted and rattled off the digits. "What are you going to tell your grandpa?"

"Let's go with simple. You and I met when I visited last year after you'd first moved here. We kept in touch and things grew from there. When Piping Hot came up for sale, I wanted to buy it and you were on board." I raised a brow, waiting for him to agree or disagree with the story.

"That works." He nodded. "And if Harley asks why neither of us had talked to him about our relationship?"

"We've both been through some shit so this whole thing feels new and fragile. We're sure of wanting to be together, just hesitant to shout it from the rooftops after all we've dealt with in the past."

"Yeah, sounds plausible. Text me and we'll do lunch tomorrow to work out the nitty-gritty." Morgan motioned toward the desk. "I'm going to work on some paperwork and then head home. Finding out I'm engaged, getting married, and buying a business all in one afternoon has me needing a beer and a nap."

I laughed. "Lucky you. I get to go face a million questions from Harley."

I left Piping Hot with a mixture of emotions bubbling

through me. Excitement, anticipation, uncertainty, and fear were the main ones fighting for control.

What in the hell had I gotten myself into?

Eyeing me as if I was a case of childhood illness he'd never before experienced, Harley handed me a beer and sat on the wicker rocker on the large front porch of his home. "You expect me to believe you and Morgan Perry have been dating and are getting married?"

I opened the bottle of beer and took a long swig as the swing under me swayed. "You can believe it or not, but it's happening."

Harley snorted. "You're a terrible liar. How did you and Morgan even meet?"

"It was that visit last year. He'd just moved to town and we met up. Ended up keeping in touch and the rest is history. He's a good guy, I like him."

My grandpa's eyes went wide. "He *is* a good guy. I like him as well. I also *like* a good cup of coffee, but that doesn't mean I'm committing the rest of my life to it." He rocked in the chair as he studied me. "Do you even love him?"

"We wouldn't be together if it wasn't right." I was avoiding, probably not well, and I figured Harley knew it. I didn't want to flat-out lie to my grandfather, but if Morgan and I were going to make Piping Hot our own, we had to jump through Jo's hoops.

Taking another drink, I waited for his inquisition to continue.

And it did.

"Why have you never mentioned him?"

"You knew Sean screwed me over good. I'm sure you know Morgan lost his husband not too long ago. We're both in kinda fragile situations and didn't feel the need to shout it from the rooftops." I cocked a brow. "Your quirky *girlfriend* forced our hand, but Morgan and I are solid."

Harley blushed and took a long drink of his beer.

"You're pushing me about Morgan, but I seem to recall that not once did you tell me you and the eccentric building owner were dating." I pointed the head of my bottle toward him. "Not sure you've got room to jump on me."

Grandpa snorted. "I'm an old man, I don't answer to anyone."

I raised a brow. "I'm twenty-eight, not exactly a child."

He sighed. "I know, I know. I just hated seeing you so torn up after Sean. You're my grandson and Morgan is a friend, I want both of you happy, but today's news almost knocked me over. Are you happy?"

"With my partner by my side and a business we both want to pour our hearts into, how could I be anything but happy?" It wasn't a lie. I'd be beyond happy once I owned Piping Hot. The fake marriage and subsequent break up and whatnot was an unexpected wrench in the plans, but we'd work it out. Morgan seemed like a level-headed man and I was sure we'd be able to find our way through the maze Jo had sent us into. "Are *you* happy?"

Harley's cheeks pinked and he nodded. "When your grandma died, I was so damn lonely for so long. My friends and the practice helped, but meeting Jo Ellen really brought me through the rough times. She's been my friend for nearly a decade, but we just recently realized maybe there was something more than friendship between us."

"She's a bit odd and very set in her ways," I said.

"She is, but she's also very open-minded, a shrewd businesswoman, and sharp as a tack." Grandpa sipped his beer. "You better believe that quirkiness carries over to a very fun time in the bedroom."

I groaned. "Okay, and with *that*, I'm outta here." Harley laughed as I walked into the house.

I spent the rest of my afternoon making notes about the business, contemplating about a million questions regarding the situation I'd put Morgan and myself in, and trying to contain my excitement. Despite the unexpected fake marriage, I couldn't help but look forward to what lay ahead.

FOUR

MORGAN

BY THE TIME lunch with Justin rolled around, I'd made a list of details we needed to work out and convinced myself there was no way faking a marriage to buy a coffee shop was a good idea, let alone was it going to work.

Jo Ellen would see right through us.

Harley was already questioning it.

Was Briarton ready for a same-sex couple to own their local coffee shop? Would they even care?

I sighed and headed toward the door when I heard Justin's car pull in.

We'd agreed to meet at my place so our conversation was assured to be private. If anyone in Briarton caught wind Justin and I were in a fake marriage—okay, I guess it wasn't *fake*, maybe *marriage of convenience* was a better term—it would be all over town within hours and our dreams of buying Piping Hot would be done.

"This place is really nice," Justin said as I opened the door for him.

"Thanks, it works for me." I'd jumped at the chance to purchase the very large, unique studio apartment when I moved to Briarton. It was a bit overpriced compared to other locations in the small town, but the renovations, layout, and welcoming feel of the place had drawn me in.

The original structure had been a garage of some sort right at the edge of town. The seller had renovated the place to be one large apartment and I adored it. I was close enough to town I could walk to work if I wanted, had a covered parking structure for my Jeep and an additional vehicle, and no immediate neighbors. The backyard was spacious with room for a deck, a grill, a hot tub, and a garden.

Inside, the apartment was bright and airy thanks to large windows. While the exposed gray brick, black and gray pipes, black hardwood floors, and black wrought-iron shelving and dividers could have been cold and harsh, I'd immediately loved the place and added my own touch of warmth with plants, candles, pillows, rugs, and books.

Upon entering the front door, the kitchen was to the left with a small half-bath to the right next to a coat closet. Through the kitchen were the dining and living rooms. The living room flowed into a little office nook. The bedroom and main bath area were open to the apartment, but like other sections of the space were divided by large wrought-iron structures. A person at the front door could see all the way into my bedroom, but the dividers gave a sense of separate rooms—almost like large, open screens between each section.

"We can sit at the table," I said.

Justin placed a container on the table and tossed a notebook beside it. "I brought some baked goods as samples."

"Perfect. I picked up sandwiches, soup, and salad at the corner store." Briarton had the best little grocery store. They kept the town stocked with fresh produce from local gardens, top-notch meat they cut on-site, soups, salads, sandwiches, and the usual grocery items one might need. While I *could* drive to the nearby larger towns for groceries that were possibly a bit cheaper, Wayne's Grocery was always willing to special order items and worked hard to keep their customers happy.

"Sounds good, I'm starving." Justin helped me carry our lunch items into the dining room and we spent the next little bit eating.

When the edge of hunger had been eased, I speared a bite of salad and spoke before popping it into my mouth. "Should we get started? I gotta say, I kinda worked myself into a tizz with all the details we need to address."

"Let's start easy," Justin said and grabbed his notebook. "Harley went for the story of us meeting last year when you'd just moved to Briarton. He seemed okay with the fact we hadn't been ready to share our relationship based on our pasts—I let him know Jo kinda pushed us into it. He's mostly hung up on *do you love him* so we're probably going to need to come across as a couple in love." He bit his lip and glanced my way. "Is that too much? How do you feel about PDA?"

I shrugged. "I'm not against it, just not very used to it. James and I never went anywhere that wasn't either super professional or stressful or starched. We held hands and hugged at home, so I'm sure I can get used to it again." Honestly, the thought of touching Justin sent little flutters of excitement through me. James wasn't touchy-feely. I knew he'd loved me as much as I'd loved him, but we hadn't had any semblance of an overly-affectionate partnership in the physical sense. My love for James had been a lot more like a very strong friendship than anything romantic—but he was my best friend, I loved him with all my heart, and I missed him like crazy.

"I'm kinda a hugger and toucher, just a warning. If it's too much, just tell me to back off. But I think it will look good to the locals and completely sell our *family* vibe." Justin finished off his sandwich and took a long drink of water.

I swallowed away the pang of disappointment. Justin's touches would all be for show. Got it. I *definitely* needed to keep myself in check and not let the set-up mean more to me than it should. Just because I was lonely and starved for touch didn't mean I could take advantage of the situation. "Something else I thought of, aside from needing to play the part in public, is living arrangements."

Justin's eyes went wide. "Oh shit, I hadn't even given that any thought." He glanced around my apartment. "What are you thinking? I can't imagine you'd want to leave this to live in the tiny guest house on Harley's property. It's decent but very small."

I chuckled. "I'd prefer to stay here. I'm guessing there's no way to play it off that newlyweds have opted to live separately."

Justin grimaced. "Yeah, I can't see that going over well."

I reached for his hand and pushed aside the zing of heat that traveled through me as our skin made contact. "Well, husband-to-be, would you like to move in with me?"

Something sparked in Justin's eyes as he shot a look at where my hand touched his and he smiled. "I'd be happy to move in here." Then he froze. "Um, so it's becoming evident I'm a lot better at planning for a coffee shop than marital bliss. Sleeping arrangements?"

My stomach flip-flopped and I huffed out a breath. "Yeah, um, seems I'm not exactly good at these types of plans either." I glanced toward my bedroom. "I have a king-sized bed—probably overkill, but it's what I was used to at my old place and there was space here, so I went for it." I gestured toward my room. "I'm sure we can make it work. It's only for a little while, right?"

Justin blinked a few times and nodded. "Yeah, totally. Just

until we make Piping Hot ours and get it set up. Then we can quietly go our separate ways and return to our regularly scheduled programming. If it's too much, I can always sleep on the couch. Not like Jo Ellen is going to know."

I winced. "Well, Harley and Jo have been coming over for dinner or coffee about once a week for a while now. It would maybe be easier to just sleep in the same bed than constantly have to make sure there was no hint of you sleeping on the couch."

Justin took a deep breath. "Okay, yeah, that makes sense. And it's not like it's forever. What else?"

"I'm thinking we need to be completely open and honest with each other if this is going to work," I said.

Justin nodded as he gathered the empty plates. "Open and honest is something I didn't have in my last relationship, so I completely agree." He huffed. "Not that this is a *relationship*, I get that. I'm just saying being upfront about things is important. Did you have specific reasons for that rule?"

I followed him with the leftover food. "I think it's just a good rule over all. Makes sense if we're going to keep up with the farce, we communicate with each other so neither of us ends up in an awkward situation with someone in town. We tell each other everything—conversations with locals, coffee shop issues, annoyances at home. You name it, we talk about it."

Justin sat back down and wrote *Rule Number One: Open, Honest Communication* on a blank page in his notebook. "Do we need other rules?"

I started to say no, but then a thought crossed my mind. "We're monogamous throughout this whole thing. I don't think I could handle the stress of faking a marriage on top of knowing we had to hide hookups and whatnot."

Justin nodded. "Oh, definitely. I'm not even looking for hookups, but I'd never put you in that situation. Fake marriage or not, I'm not a cheater. Not against open relationships either, they just aren't for me. No worries in that department." He wrote *Rule Number Two: Monogamy* on the page. "What else?"

"The only thing I can think of is we have to agree we tell *no one* about what's going on. Not Harley, not friends back home, not family—*no one*."

"Agreed." Justin added *Rule Number Three: Tell No One*. "Three rules seem like enough, yeah?"

"Yeah. You want coffee? We can move to the living room."

Fifteen minutes later, we settled in with coffee, notebooks, and baked goods. We still had a list a mile long to discuss.

I bit into a cinnamon roll. "Oh my God, this is amazing."

"Right? Definitely a must for the shop, I think." Justin smiled and licked a dollop of icing from his finger.

Shit. My libido hadn't been what one would consider *raging* since my teen years and my relationship with James had kept it very low because he wasn't super interested in sex. Ever since he'd died—and even when he was alive—I'd felt guilty at the thought of sex. Thinking about it, wanting it, getting turned on, all made me feel l like I was being unfaithful to James.

But just being around Justin had something deep inside fighting to spark to life.

Rule Number Four: No Sexual Attraction to Your Fake Husband.

We spent the next thirty minutes assuring we had a solid story and plan for the personal life side of things. Well, as much of a *solid plan* as one can have when you're faking a relationship with someone you just met.

The next forty-five minutes were spent on wedding details. Courthouse, Harley and Jo as witnesses, quick and easy. Nothing fancy, no party. The simpler we kept it, hopefully the easier it would be to end it. It really was too bad we couldn't let anyone in on our little plan and do a whole fake officiant and license and whatnot. But neither of us had anyone we were close enough to who would keep that kind of thing quiet.

With a second cup up coffee and a croissant—which, of course, was to die for—we started in on plans for Piping Hot.

Justin truly did have great ideas. And he wasn't the type who spewed plans with no follow-up. He'd done research and had facts and figures and resources to back up his ideas.

First steps for the shop included a top-notch quality of coffee and tea, a variety of baked goods, and adding soups and sandwiches for lunch.

We'd slowly move into a rotation of additional baked goods in the mornings, breakfast sandwiches, and daily specialties.

Finally, one of the ideas Justin seemed the most excited about, we'd open up the space for book clubs, crafters, and board gamers. That idea was at least a few months down the road, but I loved it and couldn't wait to see it take shape.

"So, I'm thinking we can get all of this set up in four to six months, tops. Over that time, we can discuss how we want to handle dissolving the marriage and what to do with the co-ownership part of things." Justin took a bite of a salted caramel toffee shortbread cookie and smiled. "I really am a damn good baker."

I groaned as I popped another bite of cookie in my mouth. "You really are. Good thing I already run and try to stay fit, these samples are going to make me fat." I poured the last of the coffee from a carafe. "Do you think we can dissolve the marriage quietly? Have it over and done without Jo Ellen even knowing?"

Justin shrugged. "Well, she'll notice when I move out of your house, but I think we can probably take care of the paperwork and all that before she knows. I know she's rented some of the spaces in the building, but since she's willing to actually sell to us we should be free and clear once we've signed all the paperwork."

Taking a deep breath, I blew it out slowly. "So, six months tops and then we're back to normal."

Justin nodded. "Yeah, think you can put up with me for six months?"

I smiled and reached for another cookie. "You keep feeding me dessert and I can put up with you forever."

Something crossed Justin's face, but I didn't know him well enough to read the look. Want? Regret? Hope?

"Honestly, though. Six months isn't bad. We'll be so busy with the shop, it will fly by." I sipped my coffee. "I think we get along just fine, I don't think we'll have any issues cohabitating. Hell, we'll probably end up with a good friendship from this whole thing and have to thank Jo Ellen for forcing us into a fake marriage."

"Right. Six months is nothing. We've got this." Justin shifted on the couch. "I've got a concern about the purchase."

I raised a brow and waited.

"Sean, my ex, and I dated for a couple years. The entire time we were together, I was saving for this start-up idea I had. He was totally on board. Once I had the money, I handed it over to him—no contracts, no paperwork, nothing —so he could purchase the things we needed to get our business off the ground. He split."

I winced. "Shit, I'm sorry. What happened?"

"I had no way of proving anything. He had my money and left me high and dry. Told me start-ups are always a risk and he couldn't help what happened to my savings. But I know what happened was he just kept me around long enough for me to save up the cash and then hand it over like an idiot."

Placing a hand on Justin's knee, I shook my head. "No,

don't do that. He was a thieving asshole and that's not your fault."

"Well, I was stupid to go into business with someone I thought I loved and could trust." Justin stared into his empty mug. "Anyway, depending on how Jo wants to do the sale, I need to be sure things are legit and I'm not just handing money over. I'd like to think we can either both sign as co-owners or..." he bit his lip and rushed on, "I'd like to be the one listed on the sale. I can't go through someone screwing me over again."

For a moment, annoyance flooded through me. Did this kid really think I was the type to somehow screw him over? But then I realized he was still dealing with trauma of Sean doing exactly that. I nodded. "I can see that. If we're listed as co-owners, great. If she wants to just list one of us, we'll have you be on the paperwork and you and I can work out payments. I understand your need to protect yourself."

Justin squirmed. "Thanks. It's not like I think *you'd* screw me over."

"But you didn't think Sean would either. I get it."

"Thanks."

We sat for in silence for a moment.

"So, when do you want to get married?" Justin asked.

FIVE

JUSTIN

"MORGAN WANTED me to invite you and Jo over for dinner," I told my grandpa as he watched me pack up a few boxes.

"She's champing at the bit to hear about the wedding plans and get the sale completed," Harley said with a fond smile as he spoke about his girlfriend.

"There are no *wedding plans* per se. We've got a date. Nice and easy at the courthouse, nothing fancy." I'd already taken my clothes over to Morgan's place, the boxes were things I needed on a day-to-day basis. "I'm not taking every single thing over to Morgan's just yet, just the necessities," I told Harley. "I can take other things over as I need them."

"Almost seems like you're hesitant to leave your little space here," Grandpa mused.

I shrugged. "Last time I moved somewhere it turned into a disaster. I may still be dealing with a bit of that; hesitancy seems normal." It wasn't even a lie.

"When's dinner?" Harley asked.

"Tonight. Thought we'd discuss the wedding date— wanted to ask you and Jo to be our witnesses. Then we can move on with the purchase paperwork." The rumble of an engine interrupted our conversation. "That's Morgan. He's taking a few of the boxes for me. We'll see you at dinner? I think he said to plan on five."

Harley followed me to the door. "Justin?"

"Yeah?" I turned to face him as I balanced a box in my arms.

"I've loved having you here. You've got a home with me anytime you need it." Grandpa cleared his throat. "Don't think you're going to get married and forget about me."

I snorted. "No chance of that. You'll be in Piping Hot for coffee and breakfast every day."

"Bright and early. Jo prefers nooners, so our early mornings are free." Harley winked.

"Oh my God, I'm going to pretend you didn't just say that." I laughed to myself, but fought away a pang of...was that *jealousy*? Harley—my retired grandfather—seemed to be getting a lot more action than me and had a loving relationship.

What did I have?

A fake husband, a tentative partnership, and a coffee shop.

Scoffing at myself, I opened the door to find a grinning Morgan.

Okay, so at least my fiancé was damn hot. That grin turned my knees to jelly. Seriously, the silver fox vibe had never really done it for me before, but Morgan's green eyes, salt-n-pepper hair, and devastating smile were killer and had my dormant sex drive attempting to sputter to life.

"What's the look?" Morgan asked as he took the box from me.

"Harley just told me Jo Ellen prefers nooners to early morning sex," I deadpanned.

Morgan winced and I heard Harley chuckle.

"If I had to know that fact, you can deal with it to. My

betrothed should help me shoulder all manner of burden," I teased, feeling flirty and playful. I knew we had a lot of work ahead of us—and things could easily go badly—but I was grateful Morgan and I meshed well and were on the same page with making Piping Hot a reality.

"We'll see you at dinner?" Morgan asked Harley once his Jeep and my car were loaded.

"Yep, we'll be there. Jo went with some friends to a grand opening of a winery nearby today. I'm sure she'll come bearing drinkable gifts." Harley gave a wave as Morgan and I climbed into our vehicles.

Once we got to Morgan's place, we carried in the boxes.

"I feel bad taking up your space. These four boxes can actually just be stored, I can get into them if I *need* something." I gestured toward the boxes. "I didn't bring everything, but I thought it would look too suspicious if I left so much at the guest house."

"No worries, you can put the ones you don't need in the hall closet. Your clothes fit just fine into the bedroom closet, there's plenty of room. But I can see not wanting to pack everything up now just to move it all back in six months." He helped me stack the unneeded boxes in the hall closet, then led the way toward the bedroom.

"Exactly." I started unpacking the remaining boxes in Morgan's room. *Our* room for the time being. "I actually think Grandpa is sad to see me go. He got kinda choked up and told me I always had a place to come home to." I smiled ruefully. "Which is good since I'll be back soon. Glad he's not planning on renting out the guest house; would be really hard to explain why I need him to *not* rent out the place I *used* to live."

Morgan chuckled. "Yeah, I can see him being super suspicious about that. Good thing you'll be back home before he really even has time to consider renting the space."

We headed to the kitchen to start dinner. I planned to kill two birds with one stone; I'd baked a new cookie recipe plus muffins for dessert. Our guests would get to sample future menu items for the shop.

"Hey, I thought of something today," Morgan said as he slid a dish of enchiladas into the oven. "If we're getting married, we should have rings."

My eyes went wide. "Shit. One other thing slipped my mind. I'm glad we're not doing this for real because I'd suck at it."

"No worries, your fiancé thought ahead." Morgan smiled and I nearly dropped to my knees. The man was so damn handsome and truly kind; it really was a shame the whole situation was fake.

I cocked my head, waiting for him to go on.

"I went a couple towns over to a pawn shop and found us some rings—didn't want to run into anyone at Briarton Pawn, plus they're more like a flea market and don't have as much available." He reached into his pocket and pulled out two very similar rings. "They aren't an exact match, but fairly close. If anyone notices or asks, we can just say these were the ones we wanted."

Taking one of the rings from the palm of his hand, I studied it. "This is actually perfect—pretty much exactly what I'd want for a real wedding ring." Something caught in my chest as I wondered if I'd ever get a *real* forever love. "This is solid—good for all the work I do with my hands."

Morgan cleared his throat and eyed me with a smirk. "Do a lot of hand jobs, huh?" Then his eyes went wide and his cheeks pinked as he realized just how his little joke had sounded. "Um, jobs with your hands," he sputtered, adorably cute in his attempts to tease and joke.

I laughed. "A baker constantly has his hands in something." In keeping with the really bad sexual innuendos and cute teasing, I blushed at my own choice of words. "I wash my hands a lot, too." Holding up the ring, I huffed. "All bad banter aside, this ring works perfectly. What do I owe you?"

"Don't worry about it. I got a ridiculous deal. Consider it my contribution to our new partnership. You're bringing a lot of knowledge along with baked goods. The least I can do is provide the rings for our wedding." Morgan winked as he slipped the rings back in his pocket. "I'll make sure we have these at the courthouse."

"Thank you for taking care of that." I scowled as I thought over his words. "And I think you bring a lot more to this whole situation than you realize."

Morgan scoffed. "What? My love of coffee and desserts?"

I placed the muffins on a cute display rack and the cookies onto a plate. "You've got a very positive presence for one thing. You worked a highly stressful job for a very long time, so I'd assume you're good under pressure and able to make quick decisions."

"Not that I *want* to do *any* of that anymore so let's keep the pressure and quick decisions to a minimum—I moved here to escape that," Morgan teased.

"Noted." I smiled. "You know the locals. You're good at socializing—or I assume you are since you're the type to have people over for dinner. And you have a passion for our project." I shrugged. "I think you want to see Piping Hot succeed as much as I do. You bring *plenty* to the partnership."

It was weird how I barely knew the man, but I wanted him to know he was valued and appreciated. I got the feeling he didn't get a lot of that at his old job—maybe in his old life?

With dinner and dessert ready about twenty minutes before Harley and Jo were scheduled to arrive, Morgan seemed nervous.

"You okay? You seem anxious. They've come for dinner before, yeah?"

"Yeah, they've been here before. It's not that. I've just never had them over with my future fake husband here and I'm worried they won't buy it. What if we don't seem at all like a couple who's so much in love we're getting married?" Morgan ran a hand over his face.

The thought had crossed my mind as well. "Should we practice?"

"Practice?" Morgan's eyes went wide.

Suddenly, my belly was full of butterflies. "We need to be able to play the part, right? We're going to have to kiss at the wedding, I'm sure. If it was just us there, we could avoid it, but I'm sure Jo Ellen will be expecting the traditional kiss. Probably best to get the first one under our belt without an audience."

"That makes sense. And now I'm even more nervous."

"Why?" I cocked my head.

"James has been gone nearly three years. I'm far out of practice—and we didn't have the most intimate relationship even before he died. We kissed and had sex, but it wasn't often. More like hand holding and kisses on the cheek, that kind of thing." Morgan stepped closer to me, both of us leaning the side of our hips against the counter.

"Was that what *he* needed? You? Or both?" I asked, reaching for his hand and feeling as if Morgan's willingness to share about his past was a gift he'd never given anyone else.

"Mostly what he needed. James was my best friend and we loved each other dearly. We had a strong partnership, but intimacy wasn't something we shared very often. Back then, I was so stressed and busy and exhausted all the time, it wasn't something I missed. I had my best friend by my side and we enjoyed any bit of free time we were able to sneak in." Morgan's thumb ran idly over mine. "It wasn't until he died and I finally broke away from the job that was slowly killing me that I realized our marriage wasn't what people expected it to be. I'd never trade my years with James and I miss my best friend every damn day, but we weren't a romantic, intimate match as far as partners went."

I squeezed his hand. "Thank you for telling me that."

"Open and honest, right?" Morgan winked.

"In that case, I should do the same."

"Only if you want." Morgan laced our fingers together and the butterflies in my stomach tried to take flight.

"I did a lot of casual dating before Sean, but they all turned into just sex or just friends. Sean was different. He reeled me in with sex and made me feel like I was important and part of something." I pursed my lips together. "I'll never know if it was an act from the very beginning or if at least some of it was real. We had a very active sex life, but during our two years together we slowly moved from dating and going out and having fun to nothing but sex. Like, we didn't even enjoy each other's company outside of the bedroom. The sex was good, but nothing else really was. I was too blinded by thinking we were in love and the excitement over our business plans to realize it at the time." I stared at where our fingers were joined. "But now that I've been away from it, I know we didn't have a good relationship." I snorted. "Obviously, since he stole my money and ran off. You and I are kinda opposites. You had this super strong, loving relationship built on trust, love, and respect, but very little sexual intimacy. I had this fragile, rocky relationship built only on physical attraction and a high level of sexual intimacy, but absolutely no real love or respect."

Morgan eased closer to me. "Thank you for sharing. I'm really afraid I'll be bad at this, but better to be bad without an audience, yeah?"

"Yeah," I said with a smile as I closed the distance between us. The warmth and subtle scent of his body enveloped me as I moved my arms to wrap around his neck. "God, this is quite possibly the most awkward position I've ever been in."

Morgan pulled back a bit and cocked a brow. "More awkward than mistaking me for Jo Ellen?"

I snorted.

"More awkward than taking my hand and announcing our fake engagement?"

"Okay, okay, you've made your point," I said.

"And made you smile," Morgan whispered. "Even fake husbands should make their man smile." He dipped his head slightly and brushed his lips over mine.

A tiny gasp escaped me and I leaned into him, pressing my body against his as my lips sought a deeper touch. The butterflies had worked themselves into a frenzy and my entire body hummed. Angling my head, I increased the pressure of my lips against his.

With a soft grunt, Morgan's hand came to the back of my neck and pulled me into the kiss as he moved to press my ass against the counter, pinning me there with his body. His lips teased and tasted mine, his hand gripping my neck as my hands played with the hair at his nape.

Just when I wanted to take the kiss further, longing to feel his tongue on mine and explore his mouth, Morgan broke the kiss. Pressing his forehead against mine, he let out a slow breath. "Sorry, was that horrible?"

I chuckled. "Definitely not horrible. Pretty sure I'd be up for not horrible kisses from my fake husband at any time." The way my body had reacted to Morgan's touch was a warning sign I *had* to keep my head on straight. This wasn't real, we weren't a couple. We were basically business partners doing each other a favor. No matter how delicious his kiss was, I needed to remember Morgan was not really mine. Despite the ring, despite the marriage license, he wasn't mine and I needed to keep that in mind.

But damn, the man could kiss and I already wanted more.

A knock at the door broke us from our post kiss haze.

"Showtime," I said. I didn't let myself analyze the look that passed over Morgan's face. Was it disappointment?

SIX

MORGAN

I WAS a damn mess during dinner. Hopefully, Jo and Harley didn't notice or they chalked it up to wedding nerves, but my head and body were a chaotic jumble of thoughts and feelings and I needed a moment to gather them.

But that had to wait because dinner and wine were served and Jo Ellen launched into a story about the new winery she'd visited. While she chatted about the great atmosphere and suggested maybe Piping Hot have a wine spot of sorts where local wines were sold, I finally let my mind drift.

That kiss had lit something inside me. Something I honestly wasn't sure I'd ever felt. Maybe back when James and I were teens and kissed for the first time, but never since then. The warm glow of want and desire burned in my belly as I recalled Justin's soft lips. I could almost taste him still, feel the wet press of his mouth on mine.

And then the guilt washed over me.

What the hell was I doing?

First, marrying a complete stranger so we could buy a business was ludicrous.

Honestly though, it was as if I'd known Justin for years; he was so easy to be around and we meshed so completely. The fake marriage part was insane, but I truly had no misgivings about the business partnership—and I'd worked with a broad mix of people in nearly thirty years of corporate finance. I recognized Justin as someone with a good head for business *and* a passion which would take him far.

Second, developing any kind of feelings for my fake husband—who would be *gone* in six months—was dumb and dangerous.

Plus, Justin wouldn't actually be gone. We'd still live in the same small town, still have the same tiny circle of friends. I *had* to get whatever these feelings were out of my head and get myself under control.

And the biggest dose of guilt came from my thoughts of James.

I knew without a doubt we'd loved each other wholly and completely; what we'd had worked for us and was special.

But…

I'd slowly come to realize since his death—and that kiss with Justin had pushed me over the edge—my former relationship, while *exactly* what I wanted and needed during that chapter of my life, wasn't the life-altering, flames of passion, love of a lifetime.

Was James my best friend? Yes.

Did I ever want for more during our years together? Never.

Would I do anything to bring him back and return to what we had?

Pain ripped through my heart. Bringing James back would mean losing what I was slowly building in Briarton. Returning to what we had would mean placing myself back under the crushing weight of my old job.

Bringing back James would mean no more Justin.

And therein lay my dilemma.

Justin was nothing to me—that sounded harsh, but I needed to remember it. I was a means to an end to him. But his smile, his enthusiasm, and those gorgeous blue eyes had captured me—fake relationship or not.

James was my best friend, my partner from the time we were gangly, curious, questioning teens. Did he light me on fire? No. But there was nothing wrong with that. We'd had a deep, unending love for each other. Not every relationship had to be about sex.

And so, the guilt ate at me. How could I allow that spark of want for Justin to flame into heated desire? We definitely hadn't discussed that being part of our plan. And I was a widower pushing fifty—my time for heat and passion had come and gone. Perhaps I missed out on it with James, but I'd never in a million years trade what we'd had. Even allowing my mind to stray toward the attraction deep in my belly for Justin felt as if I was…not so much *cheating* on James —he would want me to be happy, cared for, and loved—but more like by acknowledging the hot flame of desire I felt toward Justin after just one simple kiss was degrading the type of relationship I'd had with James.

I needed to clear my head of everything.

Justin and I were in a partnership with an end date and a business plan. We weren't dating or looking to take things to the next level. End of story.

And if Justin *did* want more? How exactly would I reconcile the hot, passionate way my body responded to him with the more platonic, deep-seeded love I shared with James?

I let out a long, slow breath as the conversation and sounds of forks against plates brought me back to the present.

"Would you agree, Morgan?" Jo Ellen asked.

My eyes shot up. "Oh, um, sorry. Got lost in my own head for a bit. What was the question?"

She cocked her head, her jangly bracelets clinking as she artfully tucked her tousled silvery blonde hair behind her ear. "I was saying our pasts are gone. They may be good or bad, they may have taught us or scarred us. But we can't go back —whether we'd want to or not—we can only move forward. Our pasts can guide our futures, but we shouldn't live for what *was*, only for what is to come. New experiences, new adventures, new lessons on this journey called life." Jo Ellen's eyes locked with mine and I swore at that exact moment the woman had peered straight into my brain and picked through each and every one of my wonderings and fears. "Would you agree?"

I nodded. "For the most part, yeah. Just sometimes I think it's easier said than done."

A ghost of an understanding smile crept over Jo's face. "Don't I know it. I lived several years mourning my late husband, but I later realized I wasn't really living. Ron was gone and I knew without a shadow of a doubt he'd want me to live and be happy. Those of us left behind often have it the hardest as we analyze and second guess every move we make after a loss. But I know now allowing myself to live again was the best decision I could have made," she said as she held up her wine glass. "To honoring and cherishing our pasts while taking steps to brighten and solidify our futures."

We all clinked glasses and took sips of the decadent wine.

I'd missed whatever sparked Jo Ellen's little commentary on the past and future, but her timing and words left me truly wondering if she was an empath of some sort.

"Now, speaking of the future, let's talk wedding plans." Jo rubbed her hands together.

Justin and I cleared the table and brought out dessert, coffee, and the rest of the wine.

"We'd like you both to be our witnesses," Justin said as we settled in the living room. He said it almost as if he hoped the request would temper some of Jo's disappointment when she found out we weren't planning anything big.

"We'd be honored. Now, you're doing the vows at the courthouse?" Jo asked.

"Yes, next week, Thursday afternoon." I took a bite of cookie, trying to ignore the warmth of Justin's thigh pressed against mine on the couch. Men engaged to be married would sit close together, right? It would look weird if I made space between us. And the way my body hummed proved I had no interest in making space between us.

"Perfect. We can do the party that night and then sign the papers on Friday." Jo clapped her hands together.

"Party? There's no party," Justin said.

"Nonsense. Of course, there's a party." Jo waved her hand. "Harley and I had a feeling you wouldn't want to make much fuss, so we're making the fuss for you."

Justin groaned and I panicked as Jo Ellen cocked an eyebrow. Sliding my arm around Justin's shoulders, I pulled him close and kissed his temple. "Can we really say no to our family and friends throwing us a party?" I asked softly, though I knew Jo and Harley could hear me.

For the tick of half a second, Justin tensed when my lips touched his skin, but within the next heartbeat, he melted into me as if giving himself over to whatever I wanted at that exact moment. The scent of his shampoo and soap tickled my nose and I smiled against his cheek when he sighed.

"No, we can't." He turned to Jo and Harley. "That's very kind of you. We really don't want anything big; we're not a flashy, over-the-top couple. Buying Piping Hot and hitting the ground running is a big enough celebration for us."

"Well, that may be," Jo Ellen said with a wave of her hand, "but there *will* be a party. Think of it, if you must, as a way to introduce the town to Piping Hot's new owners. As the host, I'll present you as the next fabulous family-owned, family-run business in my building." She pursed her lips. "Of course, we don't want the wedding reception to turn into a grand opening type situation, so we'll save your big ideas for improvements and whatnot for later."

Justin leaned into me, seeming completely comfortable tucked under my arm and I wasn't going to complain. Sure, maybe it was all for show, but I could enjoy it while it lasted.

A pang shot through my chest. If I already liked Justin in my arms, how badly was I going to miss him when the farce was up in six months? I needed to be smarter than I was being. I'd suffered a devastating loss of my best friend and partner not long ago. I was living again, thriving, and excited for what was ahead of me—I did *not* need to set myself up for another round of hurt when the whole fake marriage ended. Plus, we'd still have some sort of business relationship that would need to be worked out, so I'd be smart to keep in mind nothing was real.

Justin waved a cookie before taking a bite. "If we're going to do a party, maybe I could do the baking? Have a selection of some of the baked goods we plan to have available at the shop? Keep it low-key, no big announcements about the business, but when people ask about the desserts, mention they'll be some of the offerings as Piping Hot moves forward with improvements?"

"Excellent idea," Harley said. "Give them a bit of a taste and leave them wanting more." He popped the last bite of a muffin into his mouth before washing it down with a swig of coffee. "I have to say, I love me some coffee no matter what, but I'm looking forward to seeing the varieties you bring to the shop. I think it will be fun to try new ones, figure out which I like the best, look forward to what you introduce next. And the great thing about it—well, aside from all the delicious baked goods and the fact my grandson is happy and living his dream—is there's always the tried-and-true regular cup of joe to return to." He stared into his coffee cup for a moment. "I think that's one of the best things in life. Living and learning, experiencing new adventures, finding what makes you happy, but always knowing—just like a good ol' cup of joe—you've got your tried-and-true to return to."

That right there was what I'd been missing before Briarton. I'd had James, of course. But our lives had been ruled by our damn jobs. We'd savored our quiet moments, but they were few and far between. He was my anchor, my calm, my tried-and-true, but we both lived with such stress and chaos in our daily lives that returning to our tried-and-true was more a blip of time and never enough.

I knew without a doubt the stress of the job had killed James and it would have killed me if I hadn't walked away. What I'd found in Briarton—and I'd forever be grateful to whatever god of fate had pointed me toward the little town—was the calm, the reprieve, the *home* I'd desperately needed.

And I wanted nothing more than to build on the feeling of *right* and *belonging* I had in my heart. With or without Justin, I knew Briarton and these people were where I needed to be. But I had a feeling having Justin by my side—even as just a business partner and temporary fake husband—would keep it interesting and make for a fun adventure.

Who would have ever thought stressed, overworked Morgan Perry would leave the high-end lifestyle, executive level job, and never-ending bustle of the big city for jeans, a Jeep, and owning a coffee shop?

Oh, and a six-month marriage to round it all out.

Later in the evening, after we'd bid goodbye to Jo and Harley, Justin and I cleaned up the kitchen.

"So, just to add to the list of things I didn't think through, now that the majority of my things are here, I'm not sure Harley would understand why I'm still sleeping in the guest house until next week," Justin hedged.

I shrugged. "I figured you'd start staying here. We're in it to win it, gotta sell the whole thing so it looks real."

"I just feel like I'm intruding on your private life," Justin said as he put away a plate and hung the dish towel on the hook to dry.

"We're getting married, living together, and buying a coffee shop. Not sure *private life* is something we'll have for the next six months."

Justin chuckled. "I guess that's true. But for real, if you ever need me out of your hair, just need some space or whatever, tell me."

"Rule number one, open and honest communication. You agree to do the same and we're good." I glanced at the clock. "You wanna watch TV?"

"I'm evoking rule number one right now by saying I'm kinda freaking out about sharing a bed—haven't ever done that—so I'm wondering if I should shower and go to bed first so it's less awkward? Or maybe doing that would make it more awkward?" He ran a hand through his brown hair and huffed. "Sorry, not usually such a mess."

My heart warmed another degree for the enthusiastic young man who'd impulsively grabbed my hand and announced our fake engagement without pause, yet struggled with the thought of climbing into my king-sized bed.

"You and Sean didn't share a bed?" I asked, thinking if I got him talking maybe his nerves would subside.

"No, we didn't live together. In the beginning, I thought it would be a good idea since we spent so much time together, but he never wanted to. I guess I know now he never had any intention of the relationship lasting—he just needed to stay with me until I forked over the money." Justin frowned. "Sometimes I wonder if it was worth it. Two years for a decent chunk of change? But then I realized he was getting free sex and eventually a pretty large payday, it was a win-win for him." He paused. "I also wonder if he was running the same scam with multiple people. I mean, he *told* me he loved me and all that jazz, but we didn't live together, didn't see each other every single day, so he very easily could have been doing the same damn thing with multiple people." He shivered. "Thank God something in my gut always insisted on condoms." Pulling himself from the talk of his asshole ex, Justin continued. "So, no, never shared a bed. I mean, we slept together here and there after sex, but not in such a domestic way."

"I guess we could have sex and then fall asleep if that would make it easier for you," I teased with a wink.

Justin's cheeks pinked deliciously and I worried he was going to choke on his own tongue as he sputtered. "Oh, um, yeah...I don't know...would that be...shit, well...ugh, more awkward."

I laughed. "Sorry, didn't mean to make it more awkward, just wanted to relieve the tension."

Justin ran a hand over his face. "Um, maybe don't mention sex when trying to relieve tension."

"Yeah, my bad." I gestured toward the bathroom. "Go ahead and shower. I'll probably watch the news for a while before I head that way." In truth, I was ready to shower and settle in with my iPad and a movie in bed, but I thought it might help Justin to relax if I wasn't right there in bed with him the first night he shared a bed with his future fake husband.

"Thanks. So, um, tomorrow we can work through some of the plans for the shop?"

"Yep. *After* we go running."

Justin frowned. "Running? Yeah, no."

I chuckled. "Can't take the Midwest out of the man, huh? *Yeah, no* always cracks me up. *Yes*, we'll go running. That's something boyfriends and soon-to-be-husbands do, right? It will look good for Briarton to see us together. Jo Ellen will *love* the whole healthy family vibe."

Justin rolled his eyes. "Fine. But don't complain if I can't keep up. I'm used to machines at the gym, not actually pounding the pavement. And once we take possession of the shop, I'll gladly take the early shifts so don't plan on me as a running buddy."

"We'll see. I can be pretty persuasive when I need to be." I grabbed the remote and flopped onto the couch. "If you're going to insist on being a crazy good baker and filling me with sweets, I *have* to keep up with my workouts just so I don't outgrow my jeans."

Justin scoffed. "Asking you to *sample* the goods doesn't mean you have to eat the whole batch."

When I gasped and feigned offense, he quirked his brow and smiled. "I'm just sayin'."

"Go shower before I decide to go to bed right now," I teased with a waggle of my brows.

Justin's eyes went wide. "For real, though. Are you wanting to go to bed? Don't let me keep you from it. I can shower and go to bed with you already there."

I waved a hand. "No, it's not a big deal. I'll watch the news. You get in bed and get comfy. I'll come in once you're asleep or at least relaxed enough not to mind me crawling in."

"Thanks. I know I'm being weird. Promise I won't do this every night."

"No worries. Good night. We run at six."

Justin curled his lip. "Ugh, you keep making me run at six and maybe I *will* keep you from your bed every night."

"Whatever. I know dang well you'd get up that early to try a new recipe or brew the perfect cup of coffee. Six isn't too early for a run. Be ready." I chuckled at his huffy eye roll and turned my attention to the news as Justin headed toward the bathroom.

An hour later, with my eyes drooping, I figured he'd had plenty of time to fall asleep, so I wandered to the bathroom to take my own shower. Six in the morning *would* come very early and bed was sounding better with each passing minute.

The scent of Justin's body wash—citrusy with an undernote of mint—filled my nose as I turned on the shower and climbed in. Suddenly, the image of a very naked, wet, sudsy Justin filled my mind and I wasn't at all sure what to *do* with the thought.

Thoughts of sex were something from my distant past. Exploring our curiosities with James as teens had been fun, but he'd never been as enthusiastic as me. We'd kept each other and ourselves satisfied throughout our relationship, but I'd *never* thought of sex with another person.

Letting go of the heavy haze of stress and anxiety my job kept me under had allowed me to analyze a few situations in my life I'd formerly accepted as the norm. I'd been content and happy with James and never wanted for anything in our relationship. Outside of missing him like crazy—yes, every day *did* get a tiny bit less painful, but I didn't think there would ever be a day when I didn't *miss* the man I'd grown up with and spent so many years with— I'd recognized how much I'd changed once I moved to Briarton.

Was it just the town? The people? Being free of my old job? Probably a solid combination of everything.

But I'd noticed I laughed easier, took things as they came with a lot more ease, and appreciated the good in my life with more depth. Losing James and freeing myself from a hellish job had shown me the importance of doing all those things.

So, what did any of that have to do with a middle-aged man standing naked in a shower while he sniffed another man's body wash? Absolutely nothing...or maybe absolutely everything. All I knew was I was confused as hell over the weird feelings crushing my chest and bouncing around in my head. The way my body reacted to Justin's lips on mine, to the heat of him in my arms, to the scent of his soap had me questioning everything I thought I knew about my libido and level of desire for intimacy.

It was a moot point because Justin and I weren't really together and I needed to remember any public displays of affection—no matter how good they felt—were just for show. But *if* the feelings of attraction were to be reciprocated and something happened between us, would I be betraying what I had with James?

Would acting on the flame in my belly and participating in a much more passionate sexual intimacy with Justin than I ever had with James be unfaithful and degrading to the memory of what we'd shared for nearly thirty years?

I huffed at myself, recognizing how ridiculous it was to play the what if game. There was no reason to entertain the questions because they'd never come to fruition. And that was definitely for the best because I had no idea how I'd reconcile what I suspected would be a fiery passion with Justin with the solid, content, comfortable warmth I'd shared with James.

I didn't want to compare the two because I was afraid of what doing so would do to my head and my heart.

It was best to just focus on our six-month farce and being the best coffee shop co-owner I was able to be. At the end of our one hundred eighty days, we'd quietly dissolve our fake marriage and move on to being...what? Continue to be co-owners? Business partners? Friends?

I honestly had no clue, but we had six months to figure that out.

For the time being, I needed to get my head on straight, ignore the thrum of interest in my cock I was definitely unaccustomed to, and go to bed.

My dick protested the thought and twitched to life, beginning a low-key begging to be touched. I attempted to distract myself by letting the hot water cascade over my face. I wasn't some horny teen anymore. I'd jacked off plenty of times from puberty and throughout my time with James. Why had my unused cock decided *now* was the time to find a new lease on life? I was nearing fifty, a widower, and faking a relationship with a man half my age. I had absolutely no reason to be considering jerking off in the shower just because Justin's body wash had pinged my libido and had me imagining him naked.

Good Lord, man, you're almost fifty, not dead. Damn, Harley *is getting more action than you.*

Despite the guilt and uncertainty at war with my desire, I soaped my hand and gripped my cock. Feeling pleasure and finding satisfaction with myself wasn't a bad thing and I knew that. My hesitancy came from two sources. One, I worried I'd lose my mind and allow my pleasure and desire to focus on Justin. Two, I was scared to experience anything sexual outside of James. I had a lot of unpacking of that quandary to do, but I knew the basis of my fear was I'd find something *more* and *better* with Justin and feel I was saying what I'd had with James had been *less* or *bad.*

Maybe you could find it's just different. Different isn't good or bad, more or less, it's just different.

I pushed away all of my distracting and guilt-inducing thoughts and focused only on the slick slide of my cock through my tight fist. Leaning my arm and head against the cool, wet tile, the scent of Justin all around me, I stroked myself until my balls drew up tight and I shot my release in long, thick ropes that spilled down the wall.

I most definitely didn't allow an image of Justin's blue eyes, dimpled smile, and tight ass to invade my head as I came.

SEVEN
JUSTIN

FOR THE NEXT WEEK, I learned to adjust to a few new things.

First, I learned I was a major cuddler in bed. Which I wouldn't count as a problem normally, but when it meant I was waking up plastered to my future fake husband several times a night, it was definitely an issue.

Every time I found myself curled into Morgan's warm, comforting body, I immediately moved away. But I always found my way back. It seemed I could mostly reposition myself without Morgan waking, but I feared the morning he'd wake with me stuck to him like glue with a massive hard-on. How exactly was I going to explain that one?

It was one thing to know we needed to put on a show in public. Something completely different to try to reason away any kind of private intimacy.

Second, I found I actually looked forward to running with Morgan. I wasn't in terrible shape so I was mostly able to keep up and he took it slow for me the first couple days. My body, which had always preferred early mornings, awakened each day ready to tackle our run and the business. I felt better than I had in a very long time—whether from the exercise, the gorgeous views, the company, or a solid combination of all three—and I had to admit Morgan's morning runs were quickly becoming a favorite part of my day.

Which made a strange pang travel through my chest. When our marriage of convenience dissolved, would we still be friends? Still go on early morning runs? One thing was for sure, my bed back at the guest house would never be as warm and comfortable as the bed I shared with Morgan.

I shook the thoughts from my head as we turned around halfway through our three miles. Morgan's apartment was just at the edge of Briarton. If we ran one direction, we ended up smack dab in the middle of the little town hub. If we ran the opposite direction, we ended up in our own little corner of nature.

The town had installed an asphalt path from one end of town to the other and we were able to stay mostly on that as we ran. Only the last little bit before we turned around was on bare grass, but luckily it was fairly smooth ground.

"Look." Morgan gestured toward an open field.

I turned and saw the momma deer and her baby we'd seen almost every day for the past week. "I think the baby is even bigger today than yesterday. You think they stay in that wood line?"

"Probably. It's a good location. There's a creek and it's bordered by two fields for food." Morgan paused our movement by a little bench along the pathway and stretched.

Once we'd both had a moment to catch our breath, we continued on our way, the deer never once taking notice. I loved that everything around us was so peaceful and calm they could eat to their hearts' content on the quiet morning.

"You ready for today?" Morgan asked.

"Yeah? No? I don't really know." My heart caught in my

throat as I thought about the fact we were getting married later that day.

Morgan seemed to understand I wasn't in a position to explain my jumbled thoughts and let it go as we jogged back toward the house in a comfortable silence. I'd learned a lot about my betrothed over the last week and I knew he would revisit the question if only to keep the lines of communication open.

I knew without a shadow of a doubt I was marrying—even if just temporarily—one of the kindest, most generous, intelligent, and funny men I'd ever had the pleasure of knowing. Morgan was a mixture of uncertainty within himself and complete confidence with others. He'd turned into my biggest cheerleader as we discussed our plans for Piping Hot. He was also awkward as fuck at times which was adorably cute as he stumbled through jokes and questioned himself—almost as if he was reawakening and learning what made him smile and laugh. He'd accepted me into his space with open arms and we'd adjusted to our fake domesticity with ease.

We split chores, respected each other's work time, discussed issues both business and personal, and truly enjoyed each other's company. If we didn't *know* for a fact our marriage only had to last for six months or so, I'd have no problem spending more time with him.

Our relationship could have been the most uncomfortable, tension-filled situation of our lives, but Morgan and I meshed quite easily and I was so grateful of that fact.

I knew we'd have some challenges and obstacles, especially as we neared the end of our six months, but I hoped we'd continue to be friends when all was said and done.

We slowed to a walk to cool down the last little bit before we reached the house.

"I say we shower and relax, eat lunch, nap, and then get ready for the courthouse," Morgan said as his breathing returned to normal.

"Perfect. We still doing shirt and tie?" I asked, grateful I wasn't huffing and puffing as much as I had been a week ago.

"Yeah, I think so, don't you?"

"Probably for the best. Nothing too dressy, but at least nice enough to show we've thought it through and want to look good at our wedding." I took a long drink of water as I turned off the run tracker on my phone. "I'm glad Jo decided to have the party at Harley's place right after the wedding. Not sure I want to just hang around waiting for a party we don't even really deserve."

"Is it bad I'm kinda hoping the whole thing will be over in time for us to watch the early news and head to bed?" Morgan asked. "Don't get me wrong, I think it's nice they're throwing us a party, but I feel bad we're lying to them."

"I get it. I think it's best to look at it as a get together of family and friends and not focus on the fact we're lying. Plus, while we *are* lying in a way, we actually *are* getting married and we *are* partners. No one needs to know we're going to call it quits down the road." I kicked off my running shoes on the rug by the door.

"True. And I guess it's no different than people who get married and divorced every day. We just happen to have an end date in mind while others go into it thinking it will last forever." Morgan tossed his empty water bottle into the recycling tub and lifted his shirt to wipe the sweat from his brow.

The flash of his stomach—bare skin, the soft remnants of what likely used to be a six-pack, covered in a splattering of brown and silver hair with a tempting trail leading below his waistband—set butterflies aflight in my stomach and had my tongue feeling thick as I attempted to swallow and look away.

Morgan was absolutely gorgeous and I often found myself mourning the fact I'd thrown us into our particular situation because I thought *maybe* we could have had something real if our whole fake marriage thing wasn't in the way.

Instead, I had to pretend to be in love with him while people were around, pretend *not* to be attracted to him when we were by ourselves, and bite back my moans when I jacked off in the shower with the image of Morgan sucking my cock.

"Go grab your shower. I'm going to wash my hands and do the final bits of prep on the desserts first," I told him.

Once I had three types of cookies, two different cupcakes, a batch of tarts, and four dozen cake pops finished and packed for transport, I headed to the shower.

Showering after Morgan was always a mindfuck. On one hand, it was just the scent of his shampoo and body wash, nothing to get worked up over. On the other hand, the lingering scents had me hard and imagining things I shouldn't every single time. I'd seen him without a shirt. I'd caught glimpses as he pulled on a pair of pants. I'd nearly swallowed my tongue the one time he donned a pair of gray sweatpants—he wasn't packing what most romance novels would lead you to believe every leading man should be, but the shadowy imprint proved he was perfect and plenty. So, while I'd not seen him completely naked, I had a pretty decent idea of what his body looked like. And that image fueled me throughout almost every single shower as the scent of him clung to the steamy air.

Best case scenario was to be the first person showering or get in so long after him that the scent had dissipated. On the days when that didn't happen, I found myself with my hand wrapped around my throbbing wet dick as I pictured him on his knees for me as I fed him my cock. Or his hips thrusting as his dick slid between my lips. Attempting to stick to some sort of sense of propriety with my future fake husband, I kept my imagination to oral activities only—because gagging on each other's cocks was completely proper—but even the somewhat tamer images in my head never failed to have me blowing my load all over the tile wall.

My wedding day was no different and I flopped onto the couch next to Morgan completely sated after a good run and *very* satisfying shower. "Wanna watch something?"

Morgan nodded and pointed the remote at the TV. We'd stumbled across an older show earlier in the week that had us both intrigued. This group of people spread out all over the world were all connected to each other by their minds. They could see and hear what the others were thinking, feeling, experiencing. There were good guys and bad guys, a bit of mystery, a lot of action, and romance. The premise was great and we were hooked—albeit bummed to know the show only had two seasons and a movie-length finale.

We settled in and watched a couple episodes before my drowsiness became too much. When my head dropped to Morgan's shoulder, I jerked away. "Sorry."

"It's fine. Set an alarm and let's sleep." Morgan turned the TV volume down and stuffed a pillow under his head as he snuggled into one side of the couch.

I turned on an alarm that would give us plenty of time to eat lunch and leisurely get ready for the wedding before grabbing a pillow for myself and cuddling into my own side of the couch.

Morgan was just shy of six foot and my five feet nine inches weren't exactly short, so we took up plenty of space on the sofa. Our knees, calves, and feet had no chance of not touching, but the contact was comfortable and not at all unwelcome.

When I woke some time later, wondering how much

longer I could snooze until the alarm, it took me a moment to realize Morgan was holding my foot and digging his thumb into the tight muscles.

I groaned at the pleasurable feeling.

"Feel good?" Morgan asked quietly.

"Like heaven. Oh my God, so good." Another moan escaped me as he continued to rub my foot.

"I couldn't really sleep. Your foot was all bunched up like it needed to relax," Morgan said.

In unspoken agreement, we shifted our positions until my legs and feet were between his legs and resting on his stomach. His legs encased mine, his feet hitting my stomach if he bent his knees and wrapped his legs around my torso.

"You have a problem with feet?" Morgan teased as his socked toes wriggled in front of me.

"As long as you keep rubbing *my* feet, I have zero problems with yours." I took his foot in my hands and began to knead out the tight muscles, but I lost focus every time his massaging thumbs worked deeper into my heels, arches, and toes. "Sorry, I'm not as good at this as you are."

"Feels good," Morgan murmured.

We silently rubbed each other's feet for several moments —silent except for the unintentional moans that escaped me —until Morgan's touch morphed from deep to soft and gentle. I mirrored the change and studied him.

"You okay?" I asked. It seemed as if Morgan had disappeared into a memory.

He blinked and shook his head. "Yeah, sorry. Just remembering James had a deep disgust of feet. Totally squicked him out to see bare feet, touch feet, talk about feet."

I smiled and continued to rub gentle circles on the fleshy part right under his toes. "And you have some sort of foot fetish?"

Morgan snorted. "No, nothing like that. Just sometimes a foot rub feels nice and James was *never* down for it. He didn't want his own feet touched and *no way* was he touching mine."

"No footsie under the table? No rubbing cold feet in bed?" Not that I'd done any of those things either, they just seemed like things a married couple would do.

"Hardly. James was my rock, my best friend, we knew each other for over thirty years, but he was not a touchy-feely man. And feet were definitely off-limits." Morgan massaged my feet for another moment and I wanted to ask more about his relationship with James, but it felt like prying I had no right to do.

He shared with me from time-to-time and I needed to be okay with that. Delving into questions about his past with James wasn't my place—maybe I would have felt differently if Morgan and I were truly in love and marrying for real. I had a ton of questions, but mainly I wondered just how...*deprived* wasn't the right word because that made it sound like Morgan had missed out and I knew very well he'd loved James wholeheartedly. I think I mostly wondered if Morgan's level of intimacy with James was what he wanted and needed or if he tempered his desires to match the man he loved.

The way Morgan had kissed me hinted perhaps he had a lot of pent-up passion buried deep, but we were marrying for show—simply a convenience, a means to an end—exploring those hidden desires wasn't what either of us had signed up for.

But if Morgan *indicated he wanted to explore? What then?*

The alarm on my phone saved me from having to analyze that question and the way it sent a shiver down my spine.

"Want some lunch?" Morgan asked as we disentangled ourselves from each other and stood.

"Yeah, I'm actually starving. I kept out a couple tarts for us."

"Yum. Chicken salad?" Morgan asked as we headed to the kitchen.

"That works. And there are still some croissants from that practice batch. They weren't fabulous, but they're definitely good enough for chicken salad."

We set to work putting together lunch and I tried not to think about how very much I enjoyed our little bubble of domestic bliss. There was no reason to get attached to this place, this situation, or this man.

"You okay?" Morgan asked me as we finished dressing for the wedding.

He'd donned charcoal gray dress pants that fit so perfectly I knew they'd been tailored and an eggplant colored dress shirt. His tie was the same gray as his pants and he held a pair of black dress shoes in his hand.

I caught his intense green eyes, somehow even more striking thanks to the color of his shirt, staring at me in the mirror as I fought with my damn tie.

"I've never been good with ties. My dad and brother tried to teach me, but it became something they laughed at me about because I never could quite get it right." I undid the sorry excuse for a knot and started over. "When I was in school, I swallowed my pride and went to an upscale men's clothing store. I bought seven ties—made my credit card weep—and asked them to tie them. Then I kept them tied and just slipped them on and off for anything through school that required a tie. Mock interviews, job shadowing, interning, that type thing." Huffing, I yanked the damn tie over my head and sat down hard on the bed. "Sean used to laugh at me when he found out about my ties. He untied them all one day and said I didn't need them. We were going to build a business that wasn't the suit and tie type, so it didn't matter." I stared at the silk in my hand. "Guess I hadn't thought about the need to wear one again for my wedding—fake or not."

Morgan pulled me to a standing position and moved us so we were facing the mirror, him behind me. "I can't promise these next six months will be easy—I'm sure we'll run into bumps in the road—but now, and even after, I'll be here to tie your ties if you need me to."

My chest tightened and a lump formed in my throat. That was maybe the nicest thing anyone had ever said to me. Morgan's words struck something deep inside and unleashed a current of warm affection.

"Thank you," I said softly, watching as he deftly tied the silk around my neck.

"Rule number one," Morgan said. "Want to tell me what's on your mind?"

I shrugged and turned to face him, loving the way he straightened my tie, my collar, my sleeves. "I guess I'm just feeling guilty. Guilty for lying, guilty for dragging you into this." I chewed on the inside of my cheek. "Guilty for faking something I always thought I'd do for real the day I found the right guy." I shrugged. "Maybe even feeling a bit down on myself that it looks like that particular dream flew the coop and took my idea and money with him."

"Hey," Morgan said as he took my hand. "There's a lot to unpack there, but let's start with finding the right guy. *Sean* was a lying, thieving asshole who most definitely was not the right guy. You are better off without him and in no way would you ever have been truly happy married to that jerk."

I smiled and my heart swelled at how quickly and

completely Morgan had become my defender and supporter. "Gee, tell me how you really feel."

Morgan snorted. "Sorry, I know it still hurts. But hurting over what Sean did doesn't mean you should be sad to have avoided that mess."

"Yeah, I get it. Mostly my pride is just wounded."

"Now, for the parts about doing it for real and dragging me into it." Morgan frowned and stared at our joined hands. "One, I'm willing to say this is real."

My eyes went wide.

"I mean, I know it's going to end, but maybe—if it stops the guilt eating at you—we stop thinking of it as a fake marriage, because *really* it's not fake, we're truly getting married, and start thinking of it as a marriage with a known end date. Yes, it's a means to an end for both of us, but that doesn't have to mean we can't make it fun and real until our time is up." Morgan took a deep breath. "As for dragging me into it, I wouldn't be doing it if I wasn't on board with the idea." He dipped his head, cheeks pinking. "Honestly, I've had the most fun ever since that day you thought I was Jo. Moving to Briarton and starting work at Piping Hot was a huge change for me—a very good one—and diving into this crazy plan with you has been even better. I never want to forget James—he'll always be a part of me—but being excited about new ideas, making plans, laughing with you, all of those things have helped me see how dark and sad my world had been for a very long time. My old job earned me *plenty* of money, but it nearly killed me. Losing James was like losing a limb, but it allowed me to escape." He squeezed my hand. "Don't ever think grabbing my hand that day forced me into anything I don't want to do."

I blinked rapidly, my sinuses stinging. "I'm pretty sure you weren't completely on board right away," I teased. "I do remember some struggle."

Morgan chuckled. "Okay, yeah, the initial surprise was a bit to take in, but I adjusted."

I brought a finger to my mouth to bite at a nail before Morgan swatted it away. I rolled my eyes with a smile. "What about the lying to our family part?"

Morgan was quiet for a moment. "I like that I can consider your family my family. My parents have been dead for several years. We were never super close and when James and I started dating in high school things got even worse. Mother and Father allowed me to live at home only until I'd graduated. They paid for my schooling—what wasn't covered by scholarships—but never allowed me to come back home. I moved out after graduation, went to college, and never looked back. They died a few years apart. I only knew about it because a sister told me in a curt letter. I was the oldest of four and my three younger siblings obviously learned their disgust of me from my parents. I have no idea where my brother and sisters are."

"I'm sorry. I didn't mean to bring up something sad," I said.

"No, it wasn't meant to be sad. I'm just saying when you said *our family* I automatically thought of Jo and Harley, not my own blood family."

"So, how do we deal with lying to them?" I chewed on my lip. "It's really bugging me to think how devastated Grandpa is going to be when he finds out it was all a farce."

"Like I said, I think we stop looking at this as fake and a lie. We consider it real and enjoy it—it's just we're the only ones who know it's going to end a lot sooner rather than later."

The way Morgan kept talking about looking at our situation as real made me want to ask if he meant making our marriage *real* in the bedroom—but honestly, he'd been in a marriage that seemed to be mostly platonic intimacy rather than sexual intimacy, so it really wasn't my place to act as if our relationship would only be *real* if we had sex.

But damn, just the thought of sex with Morgan had my dress pants feeling a bit too constricting.

"I kinda feel like all we just said here was a lot better than the vows we're about to say at the courthouse," I mused.

Morgan snorted. "I think it's best if we stick to just the words the officiant has us say. That guilt would probably be ten-fold if we started spewing a bunch of flowery vows for a marriage that's ending in half a year."

I nodded, only somewhat disappointed Morgan seemed to hold tightly to the promise of our relationship ending. Like it was his lifeline and he only had to survive until we could go our separate ways.

"Well, how do we look?" I asked as we stood in front of the mirror. "Think we'll pass as the happy couple for photographs?"

We'd dug through the few dressy clothes I'd brought with me and found a light purple shirt which blended perfectly with Morgan's. He'd let me borrow an eggplant colored tie the exact color of his shirt which popped perfectly on my lighter hued shirt. My pants were the same charcoal gray as his and I was grateful to find I still had a pair of black dress shoes stuffed in a box.

Morgan had laughed at the fact I only had black sports socks and let me borrow a pair of his thinner dress socks as he quipped it was a good thing we weren't making Piping Hot a business casual establishment.

We looked *good* together. The colors and styles of our clothing appeared to have been purposefully planned, but even more than that, Morgan and I just meshed. He was a couple inches taller than me, the top of my head hitting just under the corner of his eye. His salt-n-pepper hair, smooth angular jawline, and bright green eyes complimented my brown hair, dimples, and blue eyes perfectly. We truly did look ready for photographs.

"We *are* a happy couple. We just have a few secrets." Morgan put his arm around me and pressed a kiss to my temple. "We also have a coffee shop to turn into the hottest little spot in the county. I'm really looking forward to doing this with you."

I smiled. "I have my reservations and nerves, but I'm so excited about the shop."

"Let's go get married so we can buy your dream."

My heart soared at the thought of making Piping Hot mine and having a man by my side who had quickly become my closest friend, someone I adored spending time with, and who supported me without question. Morgan truly was one-of-a-kind.

EIGHT
MORGAN

MY HEAD and heart were a jumbled mess. Somewhere between an adorably enthusiastic young man pouring out his business plan and then grabbing my hand and declaring us engaged and the present moment, I'd discovered not only a deep need to devote myself to building something good, but also the need to support, defend, and encourage the dimpled, blue-eyed man who stood beside me at the courthouse.

The desire to see Justin smile, to listen to him bubble over with excitement about our new endeavor, and to help him understand what happened in his past wasn't his fault and shouldn't hold him back had become a driving force in my day-to-day life.

The fact that doing those things brought a sense of purpose, belonging, and peace washing over me proved I was in the right place for the current leg of my journey through life. I'd needed this unexpected change and direction like I needed my next breath, but it had taken Justin's dream and impulsivity to throw me into it head first.

Sure, I'd had my own plans for Piping Hot, but I likely would have toed the line on keeping things pretty much the same because it was easier. Justin's excitement and dogged motivation had spurred me on and I knew we'd make the little shop better than anything I could have done on my own.

My jumbled mess of a mind knew all of that to be true. The issue came into play when I allowed myself to think, even briefly, about the feelings Justin stirred in me. For so many reasons, I felt as if the feelings were wrong—ill-timed, inappropriate, and not at all wanted.

The timing was all askew. I wasn't a young guy looking for…well, *anything*. After James, I accepted the fact I'd been lucky enough to spend nearly thirty years knowing and loving my best friend. I'd be selfish to think I had the right to want more than that.

But my damn sex drive had decided Justin was the prince's magical kiss and awakened a wild wantonness I had no idea how to handle.

Which led to the inappropriateness of the whole situation. I was almost twice Justin's age. I literally could have been his father. James and I had been less than a year apart and I had very little experience with people much younger than me outside of a few nervous, overly-eager interns who fetched coffee and reports in my previous corporate finance hell.

What my head and heart were begging to feel for Justin filled me with apprehension and exhilaration. James and I had been so easy and comfortable, perhaps no fireworks and molten-lava flames of desire, but warm and happy all the same.

I was at a loss as to what to do with the feelings I had toward Justin.

And it went beyond my reawakening sexual desire.

I *liked* him. Liked spending time with him, liked hearing his ideas, liked watching him laugh and smile.

Which would have been perfectly fine in a business partnership and friendship.

But I also very much liked having him baking in my kitchen, showering in my bathroom, and sleeping in my bed.

Dear God, having Justin in my bed had proved to be the most agonizing turn-on of all. He was a cuddler and, despite the fact I could tell he *tried* to keep his distance, he ended up plastered to me most of the night.

I didn't mind it.

Didn't mind it at all.

In fact, I cherished the dark, silent moments when I'd wake with him pressed to my side. In those quiet minutes before he woke enough to realize he was touching me, I savored his heat, his scent, and the hard, heavy press of his body against mine. My hands itched to caress his skin, cup the back of his neck and tip his head to mine for a sleepy kiss, roll him to his back and settle my weight between his legs.

Instead, I warred with myself over how unbelievably wrong it was for me to have feelings for him when that was *not* what we'd agreed to *and* he was twenty damned years younger than me.

Every damn night, I allowed myself only one selfish moment.

I stole a soft kiss to the top of Justin's head before he tensed and shifted away from me in his sleep. After that kiss, I'd float back into slumber with hopes of the next time his body would find its way to mine.

I didn't *want* these feelings. I hadn't asked for the conundrum of falling for my much younger new business partner and temporary husband. Things would be so much damned easier if the physical and emotional attraction just disappeared.

Instead, they both grew stronger with each passing day

and I found myself standing next to Justin as the officiant prepared while Jo and Harley stood to the side.

Justin and I had agreed to the simplest ceremony and tried our best to explain to our family why we didn't want anything flowery or verbose.

Jo Ellen's disappointment had flashed over her face briefly, but she'd hidden it quickly and clasped her hands together, making her bracelets jangle, and exclaimed it didn't matter as long as we were happy.

Justin had squeezed my hand and I knew guilt was coursing through him.

As we'd taken our place in front of the officiant, I'd returned the squeeze and whispered. "We *are* happy." There was no lie there.

And that added to my jumbled mind.

How could I be happy? My best friend and husband was dead. Who was I to move on and find happiness?

Don't be daft, Morgan. I heard the words in James's easy, practical voice. *I'm* dead *and you're not. No one expects you to live the rest of your life in mourning.*

As the officiant cleared his throat, I pushed the thoughts away.

For now, it didn't matter.

For now, I was getting married and building a business with my *friend* and *business partner*. Justin and I were nothing more and it wasn't fair of me to even give thought to anything outside of what we'd agreed on.

In six months, when the marriage was dissolved and we moved on in our business partnership and friendship, maybe I could be convinced to dip my toe in the dating waters.

But an odd little niggle at the back of my head wondered *Why would you need to date someone else when the perfect man is right here, holding your hand?*

I clearly needed to get this over with and move on with

the business portion of our plan in order to get myself out of my damned head. I'd never felt so confused, conflicted, unsure, and...*excited? Apprehensive? Eager?* I honestly couldn't put my finger on the appropriate word, but the mess in my head over how my heart, mind, and body were all reacting to Justin needed to calm itself down and leave me to the whole reason we were in this situation.

Piping Hot was about to be ours.

But first, I was getting married.

My heart nearly clawed its way up my throat.

I was getting married.

Again.

Not to my best friend since our teen years.

Not to the man I'd spent nearly thirty years loving.

But to a twenty-eight-year-old man with arresting blue eyes and dimples one could swim in. A man with such eager excitement to see his dream come to fruition it was nearly impossible not to be drawn in by his infectious enthusiasm and just hold on for the ride.

"Gentlemen, are we ready?" the officiant asked.

Justin and I both nodded.

"Are we doing rings today?"

"Yes." I pulled the two pawn store rings from my pocket as a jolt of guilt zinged through me over the fact I hadn't told Justin *everything* behind my trip to purchase rings. It was ridiculous and selfish and made me question myself, but I'd done it and I wasn't sure bringing it up to Justin was the right thing to do. Despite our rule number one.

"Very well. Let's begin." The officiant shifted a few papers. "Are you, Morgan Perry, free lawfully to marry Justin Wade?"

"I am," I said, my voice catching and somewhat hoarse as I thought briefly about *why* I was free to marry Justin. What in the world would James think of this fiasco?

"And are you, Justin Wade, free lawfully to marry Morgan Perry?"

"I am," Justin said, the nervous vibration of his voice hopefully only recognizable to me.

And *how in the world* had a slight change in his voice so easily become something I not only noticed but cared about?

"Have either of you brought along any words you'd like to say today?" the elderly gentleman asked, neither highly interested nor in a hurry. He seemed fairly bored with the rote procedure, but he was kind and I appreciated he was willing to give us the time to speak if we wanted.

"Um, yeah, just something quick," Justin said, surprising me as he took my other hand. "Morgan, there's so much we could say here today, but I think we covered a lot of it in private." He winked and I couldn't help but smile. "I'm excited and grateful to have you by my side for this adventure. Thank you."

The officiant nodded toward the rings I'd placed on the small podium. Justin picked up my ring and slid it on my finger. Instead of feeling heavy with the weight of what a mistake the whole situation could turn out to be, the ring was warm as Justin's fingers caressed mine. The unfamiliar touch of metal around my finger didn't send guilt and uncertainty coursing through me as I'd feared it would. My mind and heart stuttered momentarily as I tried to process how *right* it felt to have Justin placing a ring on my finger.

"Morgan, did you have anything you'd like to add?"

I cleared my throat, completely unprepared as I glanced between the elderly man and Justin. Giving Justin's hand another squeeze, I said, "I think our conversation earlier *does* cover a lot that doesn't need mentioned here." Damn, how was that for cryptic wedding vows? "But I share your excitement and I'm grateful you chose me to travel on this little adventure with you." I slipped Justin's ring onto his finger, strangely enthralled with watching the metal pass over his knuckle and fall into perfect place at the base of his finger.

"By the power vested in me, I now pronounce you married. You may kiss your husband," the older man said with a wink.

Oh shit, the kiss. We'd practiced. Once. And it had been great—honestly, probably the hottest kiss of my life and *that* sent my head into a tailspin—but we'd not spoken of it since and I'd kinda forgotten we'd need to do it again. In front of our family and a complete stranger.

Just as my nerves almost forced me to do a perfunctory cheek kiss and hope Jo Ellen didn't question everything, Justin stepped closer and wrapped his arms around my neck.

The heat of his body against mine immediately lit a fire deep in my gut and had my whole self begging for more. As his hands played at the nape of my neck, my arms naturally looped around his waist. Justin's blue eyes searched mine for the briefest moment before his soft, warm lips brushed over mine.

In a heartbeat, I angled my head and deepened the kiss. Having enough presence of mind to keep it G-rated, I reined in my tongue, but that didn't stop me from thoroughly enjoying the slick, wet heat of Justin's mouth against mine.

After all, this kiss and our first would have to be enough to get me through six months of jerking off in the shower.

When the officiant cleared his throat, I was dropped back into reality and realized we'd likely let the kiss go on just a little too long. I broke the contact between our lips, but pressed my forehead against his and brought our joined hands to my mouth and kissed his knuckles.

How in the actual hell did this feel so real, so significant, and so absolutely devastating at the same time?

In a haze of want, confusion, and apprehension I signed

my name on the proper paperwork. We thanked the officiant and soon found ourselves on the steps of the courthouse.

"So simple, but very beautiful," Jo Ellen gushed. "Now for food, dancing, drinking, and fun."

With those simple words, Jo reminded me I had another chance to have reason to hold Justin and kiss him. What a very strange predicament I was in. I needed to depict in public the *actual* feelings and desires I had for my temporary husband. But in private, where those wants and desires should have actually been shared, I had to temper the feelings I didn't even completely accept or understand. Hiding the truth from others by pretending to be in love, hiding the truth from my husband by pretending I had no feelings for him outside of a business partner and friend.

What a tangled web of uncertainty and confusion I'd gotten myself twisted in. In all honesty though, I couldn't even say I hated it. Because somewhere, deep inside, I was grateful for a situation that forced me to take a breath and live. I just dreaded the hurt I knew was headed my way in such a short time.

We arrived at Harley's house and I couldn't help but smile at how breathtaking the backyard was. Jo Ellen had gathered several of her friends and they'd decorated with twinkling lights, flowers, windchimes, and eccentric hanging items which fluttered in the soft, warm breeze and added a sense of colorful whimsy to the atmosphere.

A small portable dance floor sat under a sturdy white tent where a local teen, Alex Goode, prepared his DJ materials. I'd heard through the Briarton grapevine our reception was his first real gig and he was about to burst with excitement.

Two tables sat in the shade of large old trees and held water and lemonade, along with coffee and tea from Piping Hot. Justin's desserts were arranged artfully for easy picking, surrounded by simple plates, napkins, cups, and utensils.

"This is too much," Justin whispered.

Giving his hand a squeeze, I pulled him slightly off to one side, assuring we were out of earshot. "It's a lot, but they had fun doing it. Look at it as more a town celebration and less like it's just for us. Look around, people are happy to be here. Let's just have fun." I tipped his chin and made him look at me. "Can I kiss you?"

For a moment, the mixture of confusion and heat in Justin's eyes nearly brought me to my knees. Then he blinked away whatever he'd been thinking and nodded. "The show must go on, right?" He leaned in and brushed his lips against mine.

How I kept myself from crying at the reminder it was all for show while not pressing Justin against Harley's old oak tree and ravaging him until we were both panting and sated, I'd never know. I allowed our lips to linger, enjoying the soft warmth of Justin's mouth before nuzzling my nose against his and breaking away with a smile.

"We have a party to attend," I said, half excited and half dreading the next couple hours. I understood and shared Justin's misgivings about the whole situation, but I wasn't sure how we could have possibly kept Jo and Harley from throwing a party.

A voice crackled to life on the speakers. "Hey Briarton, thanks for coming out today. I'm Alex Goode and I'll be your DJ for the party. If you have any requests, scan the QR code and send them my way."

"What's a QR code?" an older woman hollered from near the lemonade.

Alex chuckled. "Or you can just come tell me what you'd like to hear, whichever works."

"That's better," the woman shot back.

"Our guests of honor are the newlyweds Justin Wade and Morgan Perry, let's all give them a round of applause."

What seemed like at least half of Briarton clapped and hooted and Justin tensed beside me.

Alex went on. "Before we get to the music and dancing, Ms. Jo Ellen Lucas has some things she'd like to share."

Jo stepped to the DJ stand and took the mic from Alex, her flowy shirt and skirt blowing in the breeze as her bracelets clinked and jangled with the movement of tucking her hair behind her ear. "Thank you, Alex. Briarton, if you like Alex's performance here today, be sure to get in contact with him for your next event. His business cards are here on his table. We take care of and support our own and there's nothing I'd like more than to see this young man's business take off."

The small crowd clapped again as Alex blushed before starting a song to play softly while Jo spoke.

"As you all know, our very own Morgan Perry and Justin Wade met here in Briarton and liked each other enough to make it official. Morgan is a city transplant, but I'm pretty sure he's hooked on small town living after being here for a while. Justin is Dr. Wade's grandson and finally gave in to the pull of Briarton and came home." Jo Ellen paused for applause. "While we *are* here to celebrate Morgan and Justin —a welcoming, a homecoming, a congratulations all in one— I'd be remiss if I didn't mention this lovely duo will soon be taking over at Piping Hot. I've been privy to their plans and I've gotta say you're all going to love it. Our very own little coffee shop will soon rival any big chain city shop, I guarantee it."

Justin relaxed a bit next to me, his hand squeezing mine more in excitement than nervousness. Focusing more on the business and bringing Piping Hot to life was more his speed and helped him feel less guilty. I might not have known him for long, but I knew enough to know that. Justin was hard-pressed to believe in Justin—if I had to guess, I'd say that was thanks to his parents and siblings—but his whole demeanor changed when his plans and ideas were in the spotlight. Somehow, he barely believed in himself, but he stood tall and proud when it was about his business dream. Which seemed crazy on the outside, but I'd watched him enough since that wild first meeting to know it was how he thought. My hope was he would soon learn to believe in himself as much as he believed in his business ideas.

Jo gestured toward the food tables. "Help yourself to drinks and food. The tea and coffee are some samplings from Piping Hot. The sandwiches came from our very own Wayne's Grocery. And I'm sure you're all drooling to tear into the desserts which were handmade with love by Briarton's grandson, Justin. These are a few of the options they'll be offering at Piping Hot. If you love what you taste here today, be sure to make Piping Hot part of your daily routine." Jo held a hand up as if to pause herself. "Now, before I turn this into a grand opening party—and believe me, we *will* have a grand opening party for Piping Hot—it's time to have some fun. Be sure to pass on your congratulations to the happy couple, eat, dance, and enjoy."

Jo Ellen handed the microphone back to Alex as the crowd clapped.

"We're going to start with the couple's first dance as husbands. Feel free to join in the dancing after Linzy has snapped some pictures," Alex waved his hand toward Linzy Graves, the high school girl Jo had recruited as photographer. She was headed to college in the fall to major in digital arts and photography, so the teen was thrilled to be playing the role for the day.

"Stuck With U" began to play and I chuckled. "This is our first dance song?" I whispered to Justin. "How did *this* become our song?"

Justin's cheeks were a delicious pink as he dipped his

head and let me lead him onto the dance floor. "Sorry," he said. "Jo asked me for a song and I freaked because we clearly don't have one and we didn't include that detail in our planning. This was playing in my earbuds when Jo was pestering and I just blurted it out without thinking it through."

I couldn't help but laugh as I wrapped Justin in my arms and began to sway to what was possibly the oddest first dance song in the history of first dance songs—okay, I was sure there were odder songs chosen over the years, but this one was ironically funny based on our situation for sure. "What did Jo say when you announced this song?"

Justin's cheeks pinked more, but his dimples peeked out of a smile. "She frowned at the title, shook her head, and said she'd never understand kids these days."

I barked a laugh. "I mean, 'Stuck With U' for a wedding song does sound a little weird. She's probably never heard it so she doesn't realize the lyrics aren't that bad."

"How do *you* know the song?" Justin asked, his bright mischievous eyes meeting mine. "Aren't you closer to Jo's age? Shouldn't you be complaining about *kids these days* along with her?" he teased.

"You know very well I may be old enough to be your *father*, but I'm definitely *not* Jo's age. I know this song because a couple of the teens who help at the shop after school always want to change the music to something they deem *not old* even though it's usually just set to play soft instrumentals. I've heard this song more times than I like to admit."

"I'm sorry I freaked out and blurted this as our song. I should have told her I wanted to check with you first."

I tipped Justin's chin and kissed him gently. "Well, it's not as if I'm complaining about our situation, I guess we *are* kinda stuck with each other for the time being. And neither of us will ever hear this song without recalling this adventure."

Justin grinned, gorgeous dimples on full display, and kissed me again. "That was my plan all along," he quipped.

"Suuuure it was," I said. "You just keep telling yourself that. I'm glad you're a whiz in the kitchen and have a great mind for business because your song choosing skills aren't up to par."

Justin pulled back, a playful scowl on his face. "And just what song would *you* have pulled from your ass, oh great song picker?"

I paused and wrinkled my nose. "I have absolutely *no* idea."

"Exactly," Justin said. "Don't go judging me. You have no idea how panicked I was when she asked. I froze. And now we're *stuck* with 'Stuck With U' as *our song* for the rest of eternity."

Like a fist to the gut, Justin's words hit me hard. "Well, at least for six months." I hated the taste of those words on my tongue. Hated the end date. Hated knowing this was temporary. But I had to keep myself grounded in reality.

Justin's face fell slightly. "Yeah, that's what I meant. I'm sure it kinda *feels* like an eternity. Thanks again for doing this."

I held him a bit tighter and kissed his temple. "Told you, I wouldn't be doing it if I didn't want to. Tomorrow is important to both of us."

Justin nodded as members of the crowd took the dance floor beside us. "I think we should add a few things to our list of discussion points for the shop. What music we want to play for one. Also, which employees we want to keep on and hire new." He played with the hair at the nape of my neck.

"I think we should offer positions to current employees; I think a few will want to stay, but most are heading off to college so we'll need to hire new once they're gone." My hand softly drew circles on the small of his back as we swayed to *our song*. "Maybe we do something where customers get to pick the music? Like they can vote for which genres they want to hear at different time slots of the day? Or do a customer loyalty card and once it's filled, one of the prize options is picking the music for a day?"

Justin beamed and smacked a kiss against my lips. "I knew making you my fake husband was a great idea. I love all of that."

We finished our dance and stayed on the dance floor for one more before meandering to the drinks and sandwiches where we spent a while chatting with well-wishers.

Jo was disappointed a while later when we didn't want to give speeches, but she finally backed off when Harley told her, "The boys wanted something small and private. You got your party, let them keep their private words."

The reception turned out to be a lot of fun and I kinda didn't want it to end. At least out in public, I had every reason to hold Justin's hand, kiss him, and put my arm around him. Once we were back in private, I'd have to keep my hands to myself.

As people came and went from the party, offering congratulations and promising they'd be loyal customers at Piping Hot, I kept Justin close to my side. I wanted to enjoy having him in my arms for as long as possible.

NINE
JUSTIN

"GENTLEMEN, I can't even begin to tell you how happy I am to hand over Piping Hot to you," Jo gushed as we all sat around her kitchen table.

We'd been sipping coffee and tea while enjoying leftover desserts from the wedding, but Jo had a card game with her friends to get to so she'd deemed it time to move on to business.

"My Ron and I bought the Briarton building back when we first got married. He was much older than me and already well-established as a businessman when we moved to the sleepy little town. His first goal was to make the entire building ours. We spent several years remodeling, adding onto, and making it the place it is today." Jo sipped her tea as she reminisced. "Ever since Ron passed, the Briarton building has become my passion. Not the business end of it, that was always Ron's thing. I'm lucky he left me in such a prime position to not have to worry about money. *My* passion comes from helping people realize their dreams of owning a business *and* bringing solid, friendly, family-owned businesses to our town. Briarton is small, but that doesn't mean we don't deserve the best. That's why the Briarton building houses a dentist, a clothing boutique, a hobby shop, craft store, ice cream parlor, hair stylists, and a coffee shop. There's room for more, but the businesses *must* meet my family-owned requirement and be a benefit to the town." She twirled a cake pop in the air as she spoke. "As you may or may not know—I don't tend to make my business dealings public—only a few of the parcels within the larger building have been *sold*, most have been rented. Piping Hot, however, with it being the larger end section of the building which was part of our add-on years and years ago, *is* available for sale."

I sat beside Morgan, nervously bouncing my knee as we indulged Jo Ellen in her memories and humble bragging. I was about to fly off my seat, but I kept myself mostly contained despite my excitement.

The night before had been a very uneventful wedding night as we prepared for the biggest day of our married life. Morgan had laughed that the wedding night between temporary husbands hadn't been all that much different than his wedding night with James, but for different reasons.

When I'd pressed for more, Morgan had explained. "With James, we'd gotten *married* as best friends who wanted to spend the rest of our lives loving and supporting each other." A faraway look of fond memories clouded his face. "Of course, at the time, it wasn't legal for two men to marry, so our vows to each other had been spoken in the kitchen of my tiny apartment before we both rushed off to work. We'd already both been drowning in the stress of work and by the time we met back up that evening, I was exhausted and I knew James would only be interested in intimacy if I asked. We cuddled on the couch before falling asleep and eventually pulling ourselves to bed several hours later." He'd chuckled, a mix of fond sadness. "James and I used to laugh about our odd wedding night, but almost everything about our relationship had been odd from the beginning so it worked for us. Years later, when we were legally allowed to marry, we did so along with several other couples at the state house and took a very rare weekend away to visit Niagara Falls."

Our wedding night—marriage of convenience or not—had consisted of laughing our heads off about our first dance song, ordering pizza, and drinking a six-pack of the state's most popular craft beer. While I'd had to fight the conflicting emotions regarding our wedding and how badly I found myself wanting to act on the attraction toward Morgan, we'd had a good time as friends even though I was anxious about the business deal the next day.

The buzz from the alcohol was likely the only thing that had finally allowed me to calm down enough to sleep. When we'd finally crashed, I'd forced myself to curl to my side at the far edge of the bed, praying I wouldn't soon be plastered to Morgan.

My prayers were not answered.

Several times through the night, I'd migrated to Morgan's side.

Each time, I'd woken with a start and scurried back to my own side of the bed no matter how badly I wanted to stay cuddled against his heat.

The morning of the sale, Morgan and I had taken what had become our daily run before showering, dressing, and heading to Jo's house for our meeting.

Where we sat listening to Jo drone on and on about history and family and pride. I knew what she was saying was important, but I couldn't stop the nervous flutter of my heart as I worried something was going to go wrong with the sale.

"I had the space remodeled a few years ago and opened Piping Hot when I realized most townsfolk were going elsewhere for their coffee and pastries," Jo said. "I'm not ashamed to admit a coffee shop isn't my forte and I'm thrilled to be handing it over to you. I can't wait to see how you expand what's already there and build it into something the whole town will love and be proud of. I've been talking it up and I know there will be visitors from out of town who come to see what all the fuss is about." Jo Ellen pulled out a folder from her oversized shoulder bag and placed it on the table.

"We're really excited to make Piping Hot ours and see it become a huge success," Morgan said.

I was grateful he spoke up because I was having trouble trying to form words around the ball of anxiety in my throat.

"Okay, I've had the papers all drawn up. I went through our very own Charles Hanson here in town—he's been my lawyer since day one—to make sure everything was solid." Jo spread a packet of papers on the table just as my stomach sank.

Damn, should we have brought our own lawyer? Yeah, probably.

Fuck.

Would I ever learn how to handle a business transaction correctly so as not to set myself up to get screwed over?

Grandpa cleared his throat. "Despite my utmost trust in Jo Ellen and respect for Charles Hanson, I took it upon myself to have the papers looked over by my own lawyer of twenty years. He deemed them legally sound and binding as well as very fair from both seller and buyer points of view." He gave me a quick nod and a wink.

My chest filled with so much love for the man who had been more a dad to me than my own father. "Thank you."

"Not a problem. I figured you had a lot going on with the wedding and plans for the shop you maybe hadn't had time to think of legalities. Between knowing Jo would never take advantage of family and both lawyers going through the

paperwork, I have no doubt you'll be getting a very fair deal."
Harley smiled softly as he took a drink of his coffee.

"Now then, I'd like to point out a few of the main points
on the contracts. If you opt to remodel, you must discuss
with me so I can assure your plans won't affect any of the
connecting parcels or change the building in a way I don't
deem acceptable." Jo pointed at a line. "Please initial here."

Morgan and I both scribbled our initials.

"I ask you keep the business welcoming to all at all times.
While Piping Hot will eventually be yours, I have to be
assured all of the businesses in my building are inclusive."
She pointed again at a line for our initials.

Eventually? What did that mean?

An uneasy dread formed in the pit of my stomach as Jo
droned on.

"If you should decide the shop isn't for you, the return
sale will be to me and no one else." Another line for more
initials, but at that point, I couldn't focus on anything but
what Jo had said about *eventually*. A roar sounded in my ears
making it difficult to hear her words.

"I'd like to request you hire from a local pool first if
possible. Signing here today just says you'll do your best to
keep employment within Briarton before offering to those
from out of town."

I signed my initials wordlessly and tried to speak up, but
couldn't form the words. Was I once again getting ready to be
screwed over?

Jo hesitated slightly. "I have to say this last one came after
a lot of struggling. I'd be lying if I said I wasn't thrilled for
you boys to have found each other and jumped right into a
business project together. Please, never doubt that." She
clasped her hands on the table. "My concerns come with the
speed at which your relationship formed. While I'm so very
happy to have you as Briarton residents and family, and you

do fit the requirements for my family-owned specifics, I'm somewhat hesitant to sell directly into a situation which came together so quickly."

My face heated and my stomach roiled. We'd been found out and now it was all over. The dream was gone.

But why would she have us sign if she wasn't willing to sell?

"I'm not sure we're completely following," Morgan said.

Again, bless him because he was keeping me from falling the fuck apart.

"I'd like to enter into a year-long trial period. You'll rent the space, at a very fair price, for a year. If everything goes as planned—and, of course, you remain married—you'll have the option to buy at the end of the year. All rent from that year will be applied toward the purchase price. If you decide to buy at the end of twelve months, the shop will be yours free and clear. If not, it returns to me and I will refund half of your rent." Jo eyed us pointedly, trying to gauge our reactions.

A year?

Fuck.

Morgan and I had agreed to six months.

I'd promised him he'd only have to stay married to me for six months.

And now Jo wanted a whole year before we could even think about buying the shop? We'd have to be married for at least a year before we could even think about dissolving the marriage.

There was no way I could ask Morgan to do that.

"Would you allow us to discuss this a bit in private?" Morgan asked, his tone calm and indifferent.

"We're all family here," Jo said.

"Yes, but this is a change in what Justin and I had planned. We'd like to discuss the rent-to-own clause you've sprung on us." Morgan's voice wasn't rude, but I heard his frustration and I knew he was making a point to Jo.

Of course, it was her building and her business, she could make whatever changes she wanted. She had no *need* to sell, so she wasn't worried she'd lose the sale.

Jo Ellen gave a nod. "Please, feel free to use my office. Harley and I will take a walk through the gardens out back. Holler when you've made your decision."

As the four of us stood, Jo touched my arm. "Please know this has nothing to do with my faith in your ideas and plans, nothing to do with my true happiness that the two of you have found each other. I simply find myself somewhat hesitant with a sense of unease I can't ignore. While I'm not a skilled empath, I've learned to never ignore my gut feelings. I want this to work more than anything. I look forward to a date a year from now where we're signing a complete and total contract of sale." She hooked her arm in Grandpa's.

Harley gave me a look I couldn't decipher—was he upset with Jo? Angry on my behalf? Did he suspect Morgan and I had planned on a very short few months of wedded bliss? Was he wondering just how we'd pull this off?

Yeah well, join the club, Grandpa. You and me both.

Jo Ellen and Harley walked out the back door as I followed Morgan to Jo's office.

When I closed the door behind me, Morgan turned to face me with raised brows.

"You *have* to know I had no idea that was coming," I blurted.

He scowled. "Of course, I know that. Neither of us were expecting her to throw that wrench in our plans."

"I'm really sorry we went through all of this for nothing." I ran a hand through my hair, trying to keep the disappointment from my voice and the threatening tears from my eyes. "We can likely get the marriage dissolved fairly quickly. You've been here longer, so I'll move. Not back to the city, but it's only fair I be the one to go. I'll start looking tonight; surely there are places in some neighboring towns. I've got the money from Harley, maybe he'll let me keep it and apply it toward opening a coffee shop outside of Briarton. I'll be close enough to visit often so I'm hoping he'll go for that." I gave Morgan my best attempt at a smile. "I'd guess you'll stay on as manager. I won't blame you if you use some of our ideas, but I'd like to ask that you let me keep the part about having crafters and gamers being able to secure spots in the shop for their groups."

Morgan's scowl became a deep frown as confusion filled his face. He stalked toward me and gripped my chin between his thumb and finger. "What in the actual hell are you talking about? Are you backing out on this deal? A year with me is too much? You'd give up on all of our plans over a lousy six extra months?"

A glimmer of hope lit in my chest as I studied his brilliant green eyes. "I promised you six months. I can't ask you to give up your life for an entire year just so I can see my dream come true. It's not fair."

"That's bullshit," Morgan bit out.

I sighed and closed my eyes. "You really want to spend a year pretending to be my husband? A year lying to people? A year being stuck with me while you could be moving on with your life? What kind of asshole would I be if I expected that from you?"

Morgan dropped my chin and wrapped his strong arms around me, cupping the back of my head and holding me close. When he finally loosened his hold and pulled back slightly, he shook his head. "You just don't get it, do you? You talk about me needing to move on with my life, but this thing with you and the shop *is* me moving on. And I've already said we can't look at it as lying. We *are* married. I'm not having to *pretend* to be your husband. We have the license to prove we're married. So what if we add six months? What is that in the grand scheme of things? Nothing at all. We'll be so busy building up the shop, the time will fly by." He brushed a kiss over my lips—something I was getting *way* too used to and wanting *way* too much. "So, unless *you* want to back out on this because spending a year with me is too much, I'm one hundred percent on board. No backing out, no feeling stuck, no regrets. We've got a year to make this work rather than six months. It may be a blessing in disguise; a whole year gives us more time to put all of our plans into place."

"Are you for real right now?" I whispered as I cupped his face, ignoring the fluttery feeling in my chest and how badly I wanted to lean into him. How badly I wanted to touch him, taste him, savor every square inch of him.

"I'm for real. What about you?"

"Why? Why would you be willing to do this?" I blurted. "I'm sorry, please don't think I'm not grateful, I just don't understand why you'd be willing to give up a year of your life for me."

Morgan's eyes softened and he brushed a thumb over my cheek. "Maybe our situation seems like a sentence to you, but that's not the way I see it. Quitting my job and moving to Briarton were the first two most important steps I could have taken to save my own mental and physical health after losing James. Getting a job at Piping Hot and meeting new friends was also a very positive step. But none of those things made me feel like I was truly living again. I was happier and more stress-free than I'd been in a very long time. I was healthier and the fog of depression lifted. But I was only getting by." Morgan shook his head. "I could have probably kept on that way and been happy. But meeting you, getting to dive head first into your plans for the shop, having a reason and a purpose—a mission—and a partner to tackle it with? All of those things are what brought me to the point where I finally feel like I'm living again, not merely existing." He pressed his forehead against mine. "I don't know if that even makes sense, but it's the truth. So, you may see this as losing a year of your life, but I see it as the gift of a year to really live. I know what it's like to lose years of your life to situations that bring you nothing but heartache. This is not one of them—at least not to me." Morgan took my hands. "If you want to call it quits, I'll support your decision. But please don't think I *want* that. I've never been so excited about a project before and I'm completely on board with making Piping Hot ours even if the new plan is a bit off from our original." He gave my hands a squeeze. "Come on, we're business men. We're built to adjust to change midstride, right?"

I chuckled as happy tears threatened to bubble over. "Yeah, we are." I took a deep breath. "Thank you. I'll never be able to repay you for this."

Morgan grunted and shook his head. "Stop. This isn't about repayment. We're partners. We're in this together and we have one goal. No one is keeping track of what one has done that the other needs to repay."

I nodded. "Gotcha. So, we pivot our plan a bit. Twelve months and renting to own. We're good?"

Morgan gave me a gentle smile and my insides heated. "We're good. Let's do this." He took my hand and pulled me back to the table where Harley and Jo were sitting sipping tea and giving each other teasing smiles.

I glanced to Morgan and he gave me a wink and a promising smile.

Somewhere along the line between mistaking Morgan for Jo and yanking him into a fake marriage, my heart had decided making the man smile was a top mission in life and I had absolutely no issue with that.

My concern came into play when I thought about what my *body* wanted from Morgan. This gorgeous, caring, supportive, generous man—who had already been through so much—was willing to ride out an entire year with me just so we could make Piping Hot into the place of our dreams. There was *no way* I could even *think* he might want to take things to the next level within our personal life.

If I thought it was unfair to ask him to give me a year, it was doubly unfair of me to think he'd want to share any sort of intimacy with me outside of what we'd need to put on display in public.

I knew he'd not been overly intimate with James on a physical level—although, I knew they'd shared an unbreakable bond emotionally—and it wasn't my place to think Morgan would want anything intimate with me. I'd never put him in that position.

And if he one day indicates he wants a physical intimacy with you?

Clearing my throat and doing my best to push away the thought, I shot a look at Morgan. His reassuring smile and the squeeze he gave my hand sent heat throughout my body. If Morgan one day decided he wanted to take our temporary marriage to a physical level, I'd have absolutely no way of saying no. Even knowing a physical relationship would make our parting all the more painful, I knew I'd never be able to miss out on the opportunity to know Morgan in that way.

"Well, boys, have you come to a decision? We can always push the signing to another day if needed." Jo eyed us hopefully over her coffee cup. "What's it gonna be?"

"We're in," Morgan said as I reached for the pen and initialed the last provision.

Several moments and many signatures later, the paperwork was complete.

Morgan and I were the *owners* of Piping Hot. Technically,

we were renting for a year, but we were in charge and could immediately start our upgrades.

"I'm so very happy this worked out. One year from today, I expect to be celebrating again—your one-year anniversary *and* the final sale." Jo gathered all of the paperwork. "I'll have Charles make copies of these and put them together properly so you'll have a set and I'll have mine. Don't worry about rent this month since we're midway through. We'll start that on the first." She put everything in her bag and made her way to her office before waltzing back into the kitchen. "Now, I have cards to play, wine to sip, and gossip to listen to. Be prepared for a lot of business, I plan to talk up Piping Hot all across town." She snapped her fingers. "Oh! I know you've got plans of your own, but if you're interested in setting up a little wine corner for local wines, let me know. I have connections with most of the wineries."

"Sounds good. I think it's something we'll likely want to do," I said.

"Come on, dear. Let me Uber you to your card game. No use in you driving when you know I'll need to pick you up after you have one too many sips of wine." Harley held his arm out for his girlfriend and gave me a wink. "Congrats. Looking forward to seeing what you two make of this."

I narrowed my eyes slightly. Grandpa's words were innocent enough, but I caught an underlying tone that implied something more. He was talking about the shop, right? Or maybe he was indicating he was looking forward to whatever Morgan and I would make of our relationship?

Even with a year ahead of us, Morgan and I were business partners only. I *had* to keep that at the forefront of my mind. No matter how badly I wanted to take advantage of the fact we were living together and seemed to have some crazy chemistry between us, I couldn't expect Morgan to fall into a year-long fling.

We had a timeline, an end date, and a plan. None of those things included sex or feelings beyond gratitude and respect for what we were doing with our new shop.

Didn't matter I couldn't keep myself from cuddling against him in my sleep. Didn't matter I wanted to lick his salty skin and peel him out of his sweaty clothes after each and every run. Didn't matter I seldom took a shower anymore without imagining one of us on our knees sucking the other one off as I gripped my cock and shot my load down the drain.

I was in the situation for one reason and one reason only and that was to own Piping Hot and make it into something amazing. Hell, maybe I'd eventually branch out into other locations and have a handful of shops in different towns. I had a year to make Piping Hot into everything I'd ever dreamed it could be.

That year didn't include falling for my new husband.

But I had a feeling I was facing a very long year of jacking off in the shower.

TEN

MORGAN

WITH THE PAPERWORK FINALIZED, Justin and I headed straight to the shop to get started. I loved how dedicated and enthusiastic he was about our new project. Justin wasn't the type to leave the hard work to someone else, he was ready and willing to dive in and get his hands dirty.

"I think our first order of business is to make sure we have solid, reliable employees for each shift," Justin said as we walked into the office of Piping Hot. "I plan to be around much of each day, but we definitely need coverage for the busier times and times when either you or I can't be here."

"Sandy is great. She's the one who usually works the early shift and the afternoon shift." The woman was younger than me, but probably in her mid-thirties.

"She works two shifts?"

"She comes in at open and gets through the early rush. Then one of the teens take over while Sandy goes home to get her kids ready for school and on the bus. The teens work until time to go to school. I was usually covering the slow times until Sandy came back for the lunch rush. She'd then stay until the busiest was over and leave so she was home when the kids got off the bus. A couple kids were usually able to come back after school and work until closing."

Justin tapped his chin. "I think we offer to keep Sandy on the way it was working for her. She's local, she knows the customers, and you vouch for her skills. We check to see if the teens can still cover those shifts. If not, we'll hire for those." He chewed on his lip. "What time was the shop closing?"

"Usually closed at four," I said.

"Thoughts on staying open later? If we're going to open our space up for games, crafts, book clubs, and such, I feel we'd be missing out on prime hours if we continue closing at four."

"Agreed. And if we're going to have food, even if it's not a full dinner menu, we'll likely pull in folks who just don't feel like cooking. There's a real draw to a meal made for you and a fantastic cup of coffee to end your day." I liked the idea of staying open later and loved how Justin's mind was already making changes for the better.

"So, let's get a schedule worked up and the right people hired. I want to have shifts filled by the end of next week so we can start our later hours as soon as possible after that." Justin scribbled notes as he spoke. "I'm going to work on the website and Facebook page this weekend; we'll put a call-out for interviews once we know the shifts we're looking to fill. Let's put together a flyer to distribute around town to let people know we're hiring. And we need some signs for the shop so our regulars will know our hours are going to be extended."

I smiled and rubbed my hands together. "This sounds great. Am I the only one having a hard time believing this is real?"

Justin shook his head. "No, I'm in the same boat. I'm just trying to stay busy enough I don't stop to think about it until

I'm home." He turned wide eyes my way. "We own this fucking place." He shrugged. "Technically, we rent it for now, but we're in charge. Wild."

"Definitely. Okay, boss, what's next?"

We spent the rest of the day discussing our timeline and products.

Justin had done a lot of research on which coffees and teas he wanted to offer and he planned to put in an order right away.

"Down the road, I want to roast our own coffee beans right here in shop," Justin said. "But that's more a long-term goal. For now, we're switching to a much higher quality of organic, fair-trade Arabica beans and we'll grind them fresh in small batches." Justin then went on to talk about espresso-based coffee drinks, French press coffee, mocha pot coffee, and about five other methods of making coffee I didn't even know existed. My eyes must have glazed over because he laughed and told me we'd stick to mostly espresso-based and French press coffee with our upgraded light, medium, and dark roasts.

"What about—maybe not right away, but soon—making our own little freshly ground packs for sale? If people like the coffee here, they may want to brew it at home as well," I said.

"Yes, you're thinking like me now," Justin teased. "I want to do at-home packs of coffee, loose-leaf tea, and maybe even the makings of some of our specialty drinks."

"What did you have in mind for the specialty drinks?" I asked.

"I think we'd do best to have the favorites. Cappuccino, latte, café mocha, macchiato, iced coffee, flat white. But I'd like to maybe do seasonal type drinks like cold blended coffee drinks in the summer months, pumpkin spice drinks in the fall, gingerbread and salted caramel in the winter, definitely something with peppermint or white chocolate." Justin scribbled furiously as he spoke. "Of course, we'll have black tea options, green and white, herbal, the usual. Chai latte and London Fog will be regulars. But there are so many great hot and iced tea options, I think we could have a lot of fun with those. Fall to Spring, we do one special hot tea drink every week or two. Spring to Fall, we do one special iced tea drink every week or two. The ones that are the most popular can stay on the menu for good."

Justin also had a detailed plan of which baked goods would be offered daily and which would be more specialty-type items we'd have on a rotating basis.

"We'll always have croissants, muffins, cupcakes, sweetbreads, cinnamon rolls, and cookies. We'll change up the *flavor* of muffins, cupcakes, breads, and cookies from time to time. Figure out what people like the most. Throw in scones, macarons, Danish, and brownies from time-to-time. Keep people coming in for favorites and coming in to see what we've come up with for that week."

The idea of all that baking seemed daunting to me, but I could tell Justin was excited about the prospect.

Our breakfast, lunch, and dinner menus would be small, but would have solid choices. Justin wanted to use Wayne's Grocery for most of our menu items so we spent an hour building a list of what we'd need from them on a regular basis.

He'd already broken down recipes for soups and sandwiches. He wanted regulars like broccoli cheddar, chicken noodle, and vegetable soup with weekly specials like chili, chicken velvet, tomato, black bean, and French onion. As for breakfast sandwiches, he'd rambled on about wraps, bagels, croissants, and artisan bread options. For lunch, we'd have a variety of hot and cold sandwiches daily with a special each week—likely to match the season in some way.

"These first few weeks and rotation of the specialty items

will help us gauge which items are most popular and we can adjust as needed." Justin clicked his pen. "I want to spend some time talking to the customers about our plans to open up the space for games, crafts, book clubs, and such. See what their take on it is. What they'd like to see, times they'd use the option, that kind of thing."

"Good idea. I think the concept is great. Maybe even get the hobby shop and craft shop in on the deal? See if they'd each want to set up a little display here in the shop? Offer coupons exclusive to Piping Hot customers?" I wrote a note on my notepad.

"That's excellent. Networking at its finest. Let's get a solid idea of where their displays could be so we can approach them with size dimensions and what we're envisioning." Justin furiously scribbled another note. "I really do like the idea of a wine spot with local wines."

"Same. We've got some folks who don't particularly want to travel to the wineries, but I bet they'd be happy to buy a bottle if it was right here where they're drinking their morning coffee. I'll get Jo to gather details from her connections at the wineries." I made another note on my growing list of things to do.

"So, I was thinking about our usual customers and categorizing them somewhat. Tell me what you think. We've got the early morning rush of people coming in to grab a drink and breakfast before darting off to work. We've got the early morning crew who come in to sip and savor while they chit chat over newspapers and gossip—they aren't as rushed and they linger," Justin said.

"Yeah, that's pretty much the morning group. We don't really have much of a lunch rush, but we stay fairly steady throughout the day. I'm guessing later hours will keep us fairly steady. Occasionally, as the morning rush dies down, we'll get stay-at-home moms who bring the little ones in and do their best to enjoy chatting with friends. They order a decent amount, probably in hopes of keeping the kids busy, but the length of their stay depends on how the kids are behaving." I shuddered. "She's not been in for a while, but a mom came in a little bit ago and let her kids run all over the place. Bothering customers, messing with displays, playing in the bathroom sink to the point of water flooding under the door. She sat and stared at her phone the whole time." Shaking my head, I continued. "I know I'm not a parent, but it was annoying as hell. And the other parents in the shop at the time were irritated too. I'm not sure, but I think a couple of the older ladies said something to her. She grabbed her kids and left in a huff and hasn't been back."

Justin wrinkled his brow. "I don't like the idea of any kind of rude comments from other customers, but it was likely better it came from them than management. I've not been around a lot of kids, but I've heard a few parents talk about how frustrating it is when parents don't watch their kids or expect them to behave." He rolled his eyes. "My parents were crap. If they hadn't had nannies to watch me and my siblings, they wouldn't have known what to do. They wanted to drag us all over the world to travel and see sights, but they didn't really want to spend time with us. It was more a prestige thing. My brother and sister are just like them now. Constant jet-setting, traveling the world, dragging their kids—with *the help* of course—around the globe just so they can prove how well-traveled and elite they are." Justin shook his head. "It's a shame, too. The few times I've seen my nieces and nephews, I can tell they're either miserable or going to end up just like their parents and grandparents. I hate they're shipped off to boarding school and only paid attention to if my siblings need to show their family side of things."

"Sounds terrible. How did the rest of your family turn out so different than you?" I asked.

He took a deep breath. "I think Dad was wired differently from the start based on what Harley has said. Dad was always too big for Briarton, too big for the little people and places of the Midwest. From the time he was a preteen, all he wanted to do was escape and travel." Justin gave a little shrug. "Which is fine. Small town living isn't for everyone and I understand the urge to want to see other places. I think the problem was Dad always had an air of being *better* than everyone around here."

"It's so hard to picture anyone related to Harley thinking they're better than others. He's the most humble, down-to-earth guy I've ever met," I said.

Justin nodded. "I know. Dad left the day he turned eighteen, met my mom—who was from a *very* wealthy family —and never looked back. Mom and her family money fed Dad's need to *be someone*, to be better than others—they truly are the perfect match, but very much not great for each other if that makes any sense. My siblings took after my parents— the whole group of them scoffing at anyone who doesn't have millions, multiple cars, multiple homes in multiple world-wide locations." He smiled softly. "I've heard it from earliest time I can remember...Justin is the odd duck. Justin got the small-town genes. Justin can't play with the big dogs. Justin and Harley are two peas in a pod—such a shame to rot away in that little place doing nothing." Justin zoned out for a bit, doodling on his paper. "I tried for the longest time to fit in with them, to make them happy and proud of me, to be what they wanted me to be. But the fiasco with Sean was the last straw. I hated living in the city. Hated trying to prove myself to my parents. Hated trying to be someone I'm not. I'd always known I had a home with Harley, so I came to Briarton and never looked back. I'm happier here than I could ever be with the rest of my family. They don't know me and I don't know them—and that's okay. I've found my true family here in this little town," he paused for the briefest second as our eyes met, "and this is where I want to be." With a humorless laugh, he went on. "Doesn't mean my family doesn't still bring me down from time-to-time. They could show up today and make me question every single decision I've made. Make me wonder just what kind of mess I've gotten myself into this time. I choose not to be around them, but they know where I am. I swear, sometimes I think they get bored between parties and traveling and just pop up to make me miserable. I've actually felt pretty lucky they haven't come to see me since I moved to Briarton permanently. I'm sure it's just a matter of time."

"Family shit sucks sometimes, huh?" I placed a hand on Justin's arm. "Just know that I completely understand a lot of what you're saying. The city is great in many ways and I probably could have spent the rest of my life there if I hadn't been drowning in a soul-sucking job and a broken heart. But I hear you on needing to get out. Briarton was the perfect answer for me," I said.

"How did you choose this place?" Justin cocked his head.

"More like it chose me." I smiled and shook my head. "Still kinda amazes me. You know how you see on movies or in books where they throw a dart at a map and go wherever it lands?"

"You didn't," Justin said with wide eyes.

"Not exactly. Who just has darts lying around?" I winked.

"My parents, in their game room," Justin deadpanned.

I snorted. "Well, there were no darts in *my* vicinity—I guess I never really *made it* if I didn't have a game room with darts and billiards." Justin and I both laughed before I went on. "I happened to be in a bookstore one day—probably looking for some self-help book that would ease the pain and emptiness, something to save me from the desperate feelings swirling in my head—and there was a huge wall map with a sign about traveling, getting away, seeing somewhere new. For several minutes, I avoided thinking about it. Wouldn't even look at the map. Then it was as if James spoke to me from beyond and told me to get away, to save myself, to live and be happy outside of the nightmare job and sad existence. I paced in front of that map for so long, I'd bet people were thinking I was crazy. But I finally stopped, closed my eyes, and pointed my finger. I landed on Briarton."

"Oh my God," Justin drawled.

"After seeing the name of the town, it was like I had a one-track mind. I couldn't do anything other than get the hell out of the city. Submitted my letter of retirement—I'd been eligible for early retirement, just hadn't ever thought I'd do it —withdrew a sizable amount of money, sold my fancy, sleek car, bought a Jeep, packed up, and moved here. Didn't even know what I was going to find when I got here. Figured if it was bad, I could move on, at least this would be a starting point. But I fell in love with it. Spent a couple days perusing places to stay, found my apartment, moved in, and the rest is history." I tapped my pen on the edge of the table. "I'm grateful every day for whichever god of fate sent me here."

Justin eyed me silently, a small grin on his face. "What an amazing turn of events that led to the two of us being here at just the right time. Honestly, if I hadn't walked in and thought you were Jo, if she hadn't seen us together, we never could have pulled off a fake marriage to meet her family-owned requirement."

I nodded. "You're right. Things fell into place just right. Thank goodness an adorably cute, enthusiastic kid showed up with a great business plan and a lot of determination. If not, I wouldn't have a temporary husband and a coffee shop to call my own."

Justin's cheeks pinked and he bit back a grin. "Adorably cute, huh?"

I shrugged. "Don't act like you don't know you're easy on the eyes."

His blush deepened. "I'm going to have to argue the *kid* part."

"You're almost half my age, ergo, *kid*."

"You do realize though that I'm a full-grown adult and have been for a decade now, right? You get that the age difference is just a number and doesn't affect anything?" Justin jabbed his pen in my direction.

"Business and friendship wise, yes. If we were to really be married, I'd have to question my sanity."

Justin frowned. "For one, aren't you the one always telling me we *are* truly married? Two, why? Are you saying you couldn't find me sexually attractive or someone you'd want to spend time with because I'm only twenty-eight?"

I swallowed thickly. "I like spending time with you. And the attraction part wouldn't be a problem." I knew my cheeks were bright red, probably my ears too. "But being old enough to be your father is a bit strange for me."

Justin seemed to not know exactly what to do with my words so he just pursed his lips. "Well, get that out of your head. Temporary or not, marriage of convenience or not, even if you can't ever imagine a real relationship with me or not... the age thing is *nothing* and I don't want to find out you're ever over-thinking it and making it into something. Got it?"

I nodded, pushing aside the thoughts and feelings about all that was left unsaid in the conversation. "Got it, boss." I shot Justin a smirk and adjusted my notebook.

"Okay, good. Now, let's get back to business. What other ideas do you have?"

Grateful we'd steered back to less emotional and confusing talk, I dove right in with some other things I'd been thinking about for Piping Hot. "Thoughts on having a deal where a customer can buy one of our specialty mugs—

we'll need to get some of those made up—and having that mug allows them a special price on a meal?"

Justin cocked a brow. "I'm already liking this, tell me more."

"So, they have their Piping Hot mug they bring in each visit. With the mug, they can buy a meal combo for a dollar off *and* get up to three free refills of our house coffee." I'd been doing a few calculations of pricing and we wouldn't lose money with the set-up, plus we'd earn loyalty.

"If we can get a good deal on mugs, we can likely turn a decent profit with those. The money from the mugs would cover the dollar off deal. And using the house coffee is the cheapest—not that any of our brews are *cheap*, but the house beans are the most economical of what we offer. I say make the deal include the English Breakfast tea as well for those who don't drink coffee." Justin nodded as he furiously scribbled. "I like it. This is really good."

"And if they want to fill their mug with one of the specialty brews, they can. The mug earns them ten percent off a specialty brew." We'd have to put our heads together and be sure our point-of-sale devices were set up for the proper deals and pricing, but I thought we had some good plans. "Another thought, for those who don't dine in, maybe we do a travel mug option as well. Same deal with a dollar off the meal combo. Won't get free refills since they grab their order and go, but we can make sure the travel mug is slightly bigger."

"Definitely. We don't want to exclude those who are rushing off to work—some of them will be our best advertisement. Honestly, I think we should have a goal of getting our working customers to buy drinks and breakfast for co-workers. Say Tenise comes in on her way to work and, instead of buying just for herself, she's got an order for two of her workmates because they've heard about how good

Piping Hot is. So, instead of just getting Tenise's business, we also get business from Michael and Anita even though they don't live in Briarton."

"For sure. Thoughts on having two separate points-of-sale? One for those dining in and one for those carrying-out?" I mused as the idea struck.

"I think that's a very valid plan. Depending on how business goes, I'd also love to get an online ordering app set up like the bigger chains." Justin shrugged. "Maybe not just yet, but it's something to keep in mind."

"I like that idea. I think an online ordering option would keep the in-house carry-out order crew more manageable."

"What are we thinking about loyalty cards?" Justin asked.

"I like them. We hand them out like candy. I'm thinking we start old-school with the punch cards—we could have a hole-punch with a flame for Piping Hot—and each purchase gets a punch. Or do it by dollars—like every five dollars gets a punch—we need to calculate what would work best on that one." I drew a rectangular card on my notebook page. "Fill a row, get a free drink. Fill another row, free food item. Fill the third row, free specialty item. Fourth row, free drink and food item. Something like that?"

"Yeah, let's make the card a top priority and get the details worked out. Can you find a flame hole-punch?"

"Yep, I'll get one ordered today." I added to my list.

Justin paused. "We need to set up a business account so we're not making shop purchases on our personal accounts." He ran a hand over his face. "Shit like this is where I suck. How did I not think about that detail? I'm an idiot."

"Stop. You're not. We've been a bit overwhelmed with the nuptials and all of our ideas. No harm, no foul." I checked my watch. "Let's hit the bank and get that all set up. Then I was thinking we could come back here—or maybe tomorrow morning—and assess the layout? I feel like there's a lot of space we're not using to its full potential."

"Great minds think alike," Justin said with a smile. "Bank first, then lunch, *then* we assess the floor plan."

"Hey, one thing we should probably add to our list of rules," I started.

Justin raised a brow. "Yeah?"

"We don't let this place run our lives. I know we're both excited and ready to tackle our new adventure, but let's agree we'll remind each other to take a breather and do things outside of the business," I suggested.

"Good idea. Rule Number Four: Don't Let the Shop Take Over." Justin nodded. "I'm good with that."

Justin and I quickly and easily fell into a new routine over the next few months.

Up an hour earlier to get our run in. Smoothies on the way to Piping Hot—which was something Justin was *maybe* thinking about adding to the menu. Nothing fancy, just a couple basic smoothie options, but we wanted to get more of our plans in place and running smoothly before tackling that idea. Justin wanted to have a little something for everyone, but he didn't want to stretch ourselves too thin or take on so much that we changed from the coffee shop feel.

The business was running great—it had been important to us to keep things up and functioning while we implemented changes, with the hopes our customers wouldn't be distracted or inconvenienced. Within a few weeks, we'd finalized our employee roster and schedules, rearranged our layout, gotten the craft and hobby stores on board with setting up displays, switched to top-level coffees and teas, introduced the new rotations of baked goods and specialty items, and started the new breakfast options.

The next step had been adding lunch sandwiches and soups, so customers had more than just baked goods to choose from, and moving our closing time to nine in the evening. Those two additions had been easy and very welcome.

An *official* grand opening was planned for the quickly-approaching three-month mark. Maybe grand *opening* was the wrong word, but a celebration of new owners and great new changes—three months seemed a bit far out, but it had allowed us the time we needed to make sure our plans were implemented.

Justin and I spent most of our days at the shop. In a way, it was because we loved what we were doing. In another way, it was because we liked to be hands-on and available in case issues arose. Justin spent a lot of his time in the back kitchen baking up a storm—the kitchen hadn't been built for his level of baking skills, but he made it work with a few rearrangements and added features. We jumped in to help when things got busy, ran errands as needed, and took turns stocking, inventorying, and keeping up with paperwork.

The customers were the best part of the whole adventure. Without them, we'd be dead in the water and Justin and I wanted them to feel valued and appreciated. We both loved visiting with our regulars and making our occasional customers feel welcome enough to keep coming back.

Harley and Jo were in every single morning. Jo tutted around like a proud momma cat making sure everyone knew we were the best coffee shop in the area and beyond. Harley watched her with such love and devotion in his eyes it made my heart soar, yet filled me with an emptiness.

Everything was nearly perfect at the shop. Justin and I worked together like a well-oiled machine and I honestly couldn't have asked for a better business partner to work with.

Honestly, on the outside, everything was perfect at home as well. Justin and I got along well, enjoyed spending time with each other, and meshed together very well as far as cohabitating and whatnot. I'd definitely lucked out in the fake marriage department—there's no way I would have expected marrying Justin and living with him while working together pretty much twenty-four-seven would have gone so easily.

The issue came into play when I let my head and heart and body start having feelings and opinions on things. I was about to drive myself insane with keeping certain thoughts at bay. I'd accepted I was going to *have* to talk to Justin—rule number one: open and honest—but I hadn't worked up the courage just yet. We had a good thing going and I didn't want to mess it up just a few months in.

It wasn't like I expected I'd tell him I was attracted to him and maybe had some real feelings for him and he'd throw off his clothes and climb me like a tree while declaring his undying love. I knew better than to let myself hope for that. Hell, I didn't even know if I *wanted* to hope for that.

But if I didn't say *something*—clear the air, keep things honest—I was going to combust. Spending all day every day with the man, watching him bake, drooling over his ass, doing everything in my power to make him smile so I could see those dimples, all of that was bad enough. But it was the nights that were the hardest.

Every single night, Justin migrated from his far side of the bed to cuddle against me in his sleep. And every single night, he'd eventually wake just enough to shift back to his side, leaving me cold and alone. But it was the time between that had my head and body in a mess of longing and wanting more.

I'd wake to Justin's warmth pressed against me and

couldn't help but wrap an arm around him and hold him close. If he woke, I could pretend I was asleep, right? Every damned night I held him, savored the heat of his body against mine, listened to his soft breathing, and feathered kisses against his temple before he eventually moved himself away from my side.

I wanted him next to me, wanted him to stay close.

I wanted *more* than what we had. I *wanted* what everyone else thought we had. I wanted the lie to become a truth.

Which was a total mindfuck.

One, because that wasn't part of our agreement and I had no clue how Justin would feel about it.

Two, and probably what was weighing on me even more, I hadn't wanted anything even close to resembling a sexual relationship in the nearly three years since James died. And before that, James and I were our own version of sexually active, but it wasn't the same pull I felt toward Justin.

And didn't that make me feel like the biggest asshole in the world?

James had been my best friend, my soul mate, my rock. Sure, our sex life had been what James needed more than me, but we'd made it work. Maybe it was because I was so swamped with work and stressed to the absolute limit, but I'd never felt bereft or lacking.

With Justin, my entire being begged for more.

I'd spent a very happy thirty years with James and survived on very little sex, surely to God I could make it through one year with Justin. It wasn't like my libido had just woken up—okay, it *was* like that, but I didn't think I'd feel that way toward just *any* man, it was Justin who had me going crazy. But how did you tell your temporary husband you wanted to maybe take things to the next level when you both knew the situation had a very real end date?

As we neared the three-month mark and the upcoming

celebration, I found myself in the shop's kitchen on a very normal day. I was watching him bake and I *knew* I had to say something. I wasn't sure when, but I knew I couldn't go on without being honest. It was the simple, easy connection we had—truly, I felt so close to him without even trying—and the mundane day-to-day activities we shared which proved to me my feelings weren't just infatuation. I wasn't hooked on the excitement, I wasn't living for the new and unknown. Justin and I had very quickly settled into a normal, simple life like a very normal, simple couple, and yet I couldn't help the magnetic pull which threatened to burst out of my chest every damn time we were near each other.

I *had* to talk to him.

Justin had a large batch of cinnamon rolls rising and the warm, yeasty scent filled the air as I stood aside and watched him flit around the kitchen.

When I baked, I was a mess of flour, items strewn out all over the place, spills here and there, and the outcome was always just barely edible.

When Justin baked, it was as if I had a private viewing of him blossoming right before my eyes. His movements were smooth and easy as he bopped here and there, light on his feet as if dancing to a song in his head. He enjoyed every moment of baking, from the conception of an idea to trying out different recipes to pulling the finished product from the oven. And every single thing he'd baked so far had been top-notch, worthy of a place on the display shelves of any bakery in any city.

And I couldn't take my eyes off of him. The way he moved, the way his eyes sparkled, the intense concentration at odds with his carefree humming. I loved when he'd catch me watching and smile, showing me those dimples I wanted to claim as my very own. I tried not to stare, but my gaze often found its way to Justin's ass and the way his jeans fit so damned perfectly. I found myself drooling over his baked goods *and* his body, wanting to devour and savor both.

"Here, try this," Justin said as he held a cookie at my lips.

Unable to take my eyes from his, I opened my mouth, allowing him to feed me the cookie. As his fingers brushed over my lips, an electric spark snapped between us and I curled my arm around his waist as I chewed the sweet confectionary.

Justin's eyes widened and I saw him swallow. "Well?" he asked breathlessly.

Without a thought as to what I was doing, I dipped my head and brushed my lips over his. His sweet gasp spurred me on and I pressed my lips harder against his. He melted into me, parting his lips in invitation. With a groan, I flicked my tongue out to tease before sliding between his lips. Just a taste, and I wanted so much more, but a noise out front startled us apart.

Justin pulled back, breathing heavily, staring at my lips.

"Delicious," I said, licking my lips.

"What?"

"The cookie, delicious. Among other things." I winked. Who the hell was I and what in the hell was I doing?

"Is Jo out there?" Justin craned his neck to look to the front of the store.

"Huh? I don't know, why?"

"You kissed me. I figured someone was watching and needed a show. I know she has misgivings about us getting married so quickly, but I think she buys we're in love, don't you?" Justin absently touched fingers to his lips.

I swallowed hard. This was it. I should just tell him I was feeling a lot more toward him than just business and friendship. Tell him I kissed him because I wanted to, not because I needed someone else to believe my feelings for him.

"Hey, Justin? Morgan? Can one of you come up here?" Sandy asked as she popped her head into the kitchen. "The espresso machine sounds weird."

And with that, my chance took off like a double espresso.

I dragged a hand over my face. I couldn't keep this up. I either needed to man up and talk to him about how I was feeling or get everything about him out of my mind.

While opening up about attraction and feelings I wasn't even sure I understood would definitely be hard, I knew getting him out of my head would be next to impossible. For one, I lived, worked, and slept with him. Two, my lips had gotten more than one taste and I was hungry for more. I adjusted my cock behind my zipper and went to the front to help however I could.

Operation Talk to Justin was in play. Now, I just needed to *talk*.

ELEVEN

JUSTIN

I WAS in so much trouble and I had no clue what to do about it.

Okay, that wasn't true.

I knew what I *should* do about it.

I knew what I *wanted* to do about it.

I just wasn't sure if either of those things would be a good idea because both could blow up in my face and leave me with a mess I wasn't sure how to clean up.

I wasn't sure what to make of Morgan kissing me in the shop's kitchen when I fed him a cookie. For a brief second, my heart and dick had hoped it was for real. And damn, it had *felt* so very real. But then I'd realized we were out in public and Morgan probably had a reason for kissing me. Keeping up the charade of being a happily married couple hadn't been a hardship—Morgan and I got along very well and it was never a challenge to spend time with him. Pretending to be happy and in love was a lot easier than I would have ever predicted.

And you know exactly why it's so easy.

I ignored the thought as I climbed into bed after a long

day at the shop. As usual—well, despite the kiss that threatened to bring me to my knees both literally and figuratively—Morgan and I had spent most of the day working at Piping Hot. He'd gone and picked up dinner at the local mom and pop diner in Briarton and we'd shared our meal in the office while our proficient and reliable team of afternoon and evening shift employees ran things up front.

Morgan had seemed distracted during dinner, but when I asked, he brushed it off and brought up the fact he'd ordered the part for the espresso machine. The unit was old and I had a feeling it was going to need a replacement part very soon, so I was glad to have it on the way. We didn't sell many espresso shots on their own, but we definitely used our espresso in a vast majority of our drinks so having the device go down would be a blow for sure.

The past several weeks had seen all of our first-round plans implemented. The fully-extended hours and opening up spaces for games, crafts, and other clubs had been very well-received. The rotation of baked goods and various foods was going well and we'd gathered a lot of information to help us decide which items would become regulars and which would be specialties on a rotating schedule. The loyalty cards and mugs had been a big hit and the wine corner constantly needed replenished.

I was excited and proud of all we'd done.

Our three-month grand-opening-that's-not-really-a-grand-*opening*-celebration was coming up and Jo was happily helping with plans and getting the word out.

Only one thing was bothering me.

Morgan.

The man was all I could think about. Even though I bitched, I looked forward to our runs—which was proof in and of itself I'd lost my mind. I absolutely adored every moment we worked side-by-side. Sure, we'd had a few cranky moments, a few times when our ideas didn't mesh perfectly, but overall, we worked. We just *fit*.

I loved our nights at home—I knew we'd eventually *have* to start taking separate shifts from time-to-time or leaving our crew to run things because there was no way we could keep up early morning to late night shifts the way we'd been doing.

I knew Morgan was worried about stretching ourselves too thin and I agreed we needed to take time for ourselves.

Which only made me look forward to our time at home even more once we had a little more of it.

But the hours we spent in bed were perhaps the best and worst of the whole situation. Every damned night, my sleeping body somehow found its way to Morgan's side. And every damned night it got more and more difficult to roll away from his strong, warm body.

I dreamed of him wrapping his arm around me, kissing my head, whispering in my ear. And I wanted that, every single moment of it.

I knew I needed to talk to Morgan. It wasn't fair to lust over him and have all of these feelings for him in secret. We'd promised we'd give it a year and be honest with each other throughout our time together.

Maybe it would ruin the easy thing we had going between us.

Maybe it would make it better.

Maybe just voicing it would ease the throbbing want I had for him every time we were near each other.

Hell, it didn't even take being near Morgan to want him. All I had to do was *think* about the man and I was imagining what it would be like to take our situation to the next level.

An hour after I curled to my side and tried to tell my body to stay in my own section of the bed, I woke with a warmth at my back and an arm around my waist.

Shit.

Morgan was holding me—surely still asleep and just reacting to the press of a body against his.

As I tried to shift away from him and retreat to my side of the bed—my heart and cock begging me to stay right where I was—Morgan's arm tightened around me.

"Stay," he said in a ragged whisper.

"Morgan?" I asked, sure he was dreaming.

"Please, just stay," Morgan said, caressing my arm and lacing our fingers together against my stomach.

Without a second of hesitation, I cuddled deeper into Morgan's warmth and sighed. Whatever was going on, we could talk about it when we were awake. No way was I going to give up the chance to sleep in Morgan's arms.

How badly will you miss this in a year?

I refused to worry about that.

We had an entire twelve months ahead of us. Okay, it was closer to nine, but that was still a long time.

I had no clue what Morgan's request for me to stay by his side actually meant. Maybe he was just feeling lonely—hell, I knew the feeling so fucking well.

But those few kisses we'd shared—even if they were just for practice and show—had lit a fire in my belly that threatened to consume me.

We'd talk and figure out what the hell was going on and how we wanted to handle it.

I slept the rest of the night and never woke once. It was amazing how perfectly at ease and comfortable I was in Morgan's embrace.

As the sun peeked into the bedroom, I came awake knowing Morgan was watching me. "Creeper," I mumbled, loving the warmth of his skin and the tickle of chest hair against my lips. "Why are you watching me?"

"Can't help it," he answered gruffly.

We stayed quiet for a moment, Morgan's hand caressing up and down my back.

"You asked me to stay," I said.

"I did."

"Why?" I asked.

"I like feeling you against me. Like having you in my arms." He tensed next to me as if his admission was a bad thing.

"I like it, too." Oh God, how I liked it.

Morgan relaxed. "I'm sorry. I wasn't expecting this and I know it wasn't anything we agreed on."

I shifted, propping myself on my arm tucked under my head. "Not sure you can plan for attraction." I frowned. "What should we do about it?"

Morgan closed his eyes and sighed. "I don't know. I'm so damn torn."

"Talk to me."

"That damn rule number one is my nemesis. If not for promising we'd be open and honest, I probably would have hidden whatever this is for a year."

I chuckled. "That rule is exactly why I was planning to talk to you, too."

"You were?"

"Yeah, we promised," I answered with a shrug.

"What were you going to talk to me about?" Morgan asked.

My cheeks heated and I bit my lip. "The fact that I'm crazy attracted to you and spend way too much time jacking off in the shower while thinking about you," I blurted and then buried my head in the crook of my elbow. "Oh my God, that sounds so creepy."

Morgan tipped my chin and made me look at him. "Well, if it's creepy, count me as a big time creep because I've been doing the same."

"You have?"

"Yeah, the scent of your body wash does it to me every damn time." Morgan's eyes were a mix of playful twinkle and fiery desire.

"And you feel guilty about it because of James?" I asked.

Morgan nodded.

"You've told me enough for me to know you guys weren't super sexually active," I said, hoping it would encourage him to open up.

"We weren't. When we first met, we kinda had the whole infatuation thing going. It was a while before we experimented with anything sexual. I enjoyed it. James said he did, but I always got the feeling he was only interested if it was something I wanted to do—like he wouldn't initiate anything sexual. We kissed and touched *a lot* and eventually made hand jobs a pretty regular thing. As the years went on, we discovered James didn't enjoy receiving blowjobs, but he was willing to give them because he knew I liked them. He didn't enjoy penetrative sex at all, giving or receiving, but he was happy to finger me from time-to-time if I asked. He didn't want the act reciprocated." Morgan scowled. "It wasn't until we'd been together for nearly three decades I realized James was likely asexual or some subcategory of it."

"Did the sex stuff ever cause problems for the two of you?" I asked.

Morgan shook his head. "No, never. We grew up together, explored together, learned what we each liked and didn't like together. I respected his boundaries and he was always happy to do what I liked, within his limits. Honestly, once we both got our jobs straight out of college and dove head-first into the depths of soul-sucking corporate finance, my sex drive nearly disappeared due to stress and exhaustion. When we did find time for intimacy, I adjusted for him and he adjusted for me. We made it work and it was never an issue."

"But you feel guilty now?"

Morgan nodded. "I do. This pull I feel toward you is something I've never really felt—maybe way back during puberty when I was rubbing off on my sheets—and I feel guilty I never felt this way toward James."

"Maybe you would have, given different circumstances. You loved him so much and you were willing to shift what you wanted to fit with what he was able to give. Without the stress of your job, maybe your sex drive would have been stronger at the time," I suggested.

Morgan seemed to mull over my words. "And if my sex drive had been stronger, it may have put pressure on James. Maybe that was a tiny benefit in a sea of toxic negatives surrounding our jobs."

"I don't think you feeling something between us means what you had with James was anything less than exactly what you both needed it to be."

Morgan's hand slid down my arm and he took my hand in his, bringing our joined hands to his lips before resting them on the mattress between us. "You're pretty smart, you know that?"

I shrugged. "I have my moments." Staring at our joined hands, I finally spoke. "So, what are we going to do about our little mutual attraction situation?"

"Well, I came into this conversation knowing I *had* to be honest with you and you'd react in one of two ways."

I smirked. "And what were those two ways?"

"You'd tell me to fuck off, keep my sexy thoughts to myself, and to never jack off to images of you again."

Raising a brow, I waited.

"Or, you'd tell me you were just as lonely as me, wanted to touch just as badly as me, and agree to taking this to the next level for the rest of our year together."

Butterflies took flight in my stomach and had to remind

myself to breathe. "Well, I'm definitely not taking option one."

Morgan studied my face, waiting.

"Option two sounds really good, but is it the smart thing to do? Is it simply because we're lonely?"

He let out a long breath. "Honestly, I don't know. I definitely don't think I'm attracted to you just because I'm lonely, but I do have a lot of mixed up thoughts and feelings."

"Tell me." I squeezed his hand.

"First, I don't want to push you into something you don't want. Just because we're married and spend most of our time together, I don't want you to feel like you *have to* be with me in any kind of sexual capacity."

I shook my head. "I don't feel that way at all."

"I'm still a bit concerned about the age gap, I'm worried my limited sexual history will be a turn-off or a compatibility issue, and I *do* feel guilty about moving on from James."

Caressing the back of his hand with my thumb, I said, "Get the age gap out of your head. It's nothing. Jo was married to a man twenty-five years her senior. There are a million people involved in relationships with five, ten, twenty, or more years between them. There is no rule that says you have to be with a person your same age."

"You were an infant when I was in college," Morgan protested.

"And we're both grown men who are experienced and mature enough to know when we're attracted to someone and make a consenting decision as to what to do about it."

Morgan nodded slightly, almost as if he wasn't completely convinced but he knew he wasn't going to win the argument.

I went on. "Your limited sexual history isn't a problem. We have almost a year to play and explore and see what we like. If we decide to take this to a sexual level, we'll keep with the open and honest rule in bed too." My eyes met with

Morgan's. "I can't tell you when to move on from James. I *can* tell you I know the two of you were best friends and loved each other very much. Best friends would never expect the other to be sad or alone forever. I didn't know James, but I know you and I think you both would want the other one to be happy." I pulled our joined hands to my chest. "I would *never* ask to replace James in your heart and nothing we do together would ever be competition between me and him. I've never dealt with the loss of a friend or lover, so I can't say how I'd feel, but the way I see it, you don't have to forget James or compare what you and he had to what you and I might have. It's okay to move on and enjoy something else even while you'll always love and cherish what's in the past."

Morgan closed his eyes and leaned in, pressing his forehead against mine. "Thanks. A lot of that is what I *know*, deep down, James would say as well, but I think I needed to hear it from someone else."

"What else is weighing on you?" I had a feeling Morgan had other concerns and I'd be lying if I didn't have my own.

He was quiet for a moment. "It's hard to explain."

"Try."

"I've only ever been in one relationship, but it feels weird going into something as intimate as sex *knowing* there's an end date," Morgan said.

I nodded. "I definitely get that. I think that's been my biggest issue when thinking about wanting something more with you. For one, I've never been super successful in relationships," I said.

"That's their issue and their loss," Morgan interrupted.

I smiled. "Thanks. But I have to be real and say I'm concerned adding a physical aspect to what we have could screw things up completely. And it's also weird to agree to sex—in whatever form we discover works for us—knowing there's a time limit."

Morgan nodded.

"But on the other hand—and this makes me wonder if I'm just making excuses or if it's a valid thought—a vast majority of relationships end at some point, right? First love, serious dating, engagements, marriages, long-term partnerships, a lot of those end. From the most casual to the most committed, no relationship is guaranteed and a large percentage end. Most of the endings are unexpected, but there's still an ending. Would we really be that different in what we're doing just because we know the end date?"

I swallowed thickly. I wasn't being completely honest with Morgan. While I *did* want to take things to the next level between us, I had definite thoughts on not wanting the relationship to end at all. I wanted more than anything to ask if we could just forget the end date, forget this was all a farce from the beginning, and live happily ever after or for as long as we were able.

But I worried throwing that tidbit at Morgan would be too much too soon. So, I'd bide my time. I'd settle for stepping up to the next level *with* an end date and hope that maybe, just maybe, Morgan would feel the same farther down the road.

He nodded. "Yeah, that makes sense. In the grand scheme of things, I guess knowing our breakup date is just an added layer to the unconventional relationship we've had from the start. No shock, no unexpected surprises, no heartbreak."

Speak for yourself I thought. I knew, as surely as I knew I felt more for Morgan than just a physical attraction, I'd be devasted when we eventually parted ways. But the desire flooding my body wouldn't allow me to voice those feelings out of fear I'd push Morgan away and lose the chance to experience something amazing with him.

"So, just to be clear so we're both on the same page. Are we agreeing to add a physical aspect to our relationship outside of friendship and business partners?" I needed to be sure we were talking about the same thing.

"Yes, that's what I'm talking about. You?"

I nodded. "We don't force anything. Just let things happen as they happen. If it feels right, we go with it. No expectations or requirements."

"And we keep the communication open with this just the same as with the rest of it," Morgan said.

Guiltily, knowing I was already hiding something, I nodded again. "As much as I'd *really* like to kiss you right now, I'm pretty sure the onion in last night's dinner has grown claws and a tail in my mouth and I'm *not* having our first make out session be with me having dragon breath."

Morgan laughed just as his phone buzzed. He reached for it and sighed. "Well, I guess it's good we didn't get too far into something because Jo wants to meet at the shop to discuss the celebration."

"Duty calls," I said and pouted.

"Starting today, we go in an hour later and leave earlier in the evening. Or, we can alternate with taking off the quieter afternoon shifts." Morgan cupped my face. "We'd already said we wouldn't let the business run our life *and* we'd talked about giving up some of the hours we've been spending there. We have a great staff working for us, they can handle our absence."

I took a deep breath. "Agreed. But I gotta say this is maybe what a parent feels like when they consider leaving their baby with a sitter for the first time."

"This will be good practice."

Frowning, I asked, "For what?"

Morgan smirked. "After the celebration this week, you and I are taking a vacation."

"What?" I squeaked.

He just laughed and rolled out of bed. "Come on, get up.

We missed our run this morning. We'll make up for it by leaving early today and running in the evening. Then we're going to make good use of the hot tub."

"Don't think I'm going to forget you just told me we're leaving our child for multiple days," I groused as I stretched and climbed out of bed. "But I'm easy and can likely be distracted by the promise of a hot tub for at least a little while."

Morgan chuckled as we stood in the bedroom, facing each other. As if we were opposite poles of a magnet, our feet carried us closer and closer until he reached for me and pulled me close.

I wrapped my arms around his shoulders and buried my face in his neck. We'd just had a monumental discussion and come to some possibly life-changing decisions. While I definitely wanted to kiss and touch *right that very moment*, I also enjoyed just savoring Morgan's warmth and not rushing into anything. We were on the same page. We had time. A little anticipation would only fan the flames. "Will there be kissing in the hot tub?" I asked.

A laugh rumbled through Morgan's chest against mine. "Would you be interested in kissing in the hot tub?"

"*Highly* interested." I played with the hair at the nape of Morgan's neck.

"I'll see what can be arranged," he said as he brushed a kiss against my temple.

We broke apart and got ready for our day. As much as I loved my job, I was looking forward to time away from the shop to explore the new facet of our relationship.

TWELVE
MORGAN

WE WENT about our day as if nothing had changed between us. And maybe, in a sense, nothing had.

Even though *everything* had changed.

Jo Ellen, Justin, and I finalized plans for the celebration. The event was planned to be an all-day affair at Piping Hot with discounts, samples, and prizes. We'd keep the shop running as normally as possible while also celebrating our successes and future plans. Jo had promised she and Harley would be there all day to help. Justin and I would also be there. The plan was the four of us would pretty much handle the celebration side of things while our staff took care of the day-to-day to avoid disruption in service.

After our meeting, the day went smoothly and I spent a bit of time planning an impromptu weekend getaway while Justin baked up a storm. By the time dinner rolled around, I had serious doubts about being able to drag Justin away from the shop despite the fact our evening crew was one of the best.

"Five minutes," I called out as Justin rushed past the office door.

I heard him stop and backtrack before his head appeared with a sheepish smile. "Maybe you go run and I'll just finish some things here?"

I shook my head and motioned him closer.

Justin bit his lip as he made his way toward me.

Standing from the chair, I moved to meet him in front of the desk. "We agreed we wouldn't work ourselves sick. We need time to ourselves—and I'm not just talking about *us*, I'm talking about independently, too. You and I both know the shop is in perfectly capable hands. You've finished all the baking, I finished stocking. I know you've checked the inventory and put in an order. There's nothing pressing for us to do here right now." I reached for him and pulled him to stand between my legs, thrilling at the fact I could touch him without putting on a show or worrying he'd wonder what the hell I was doing.

Justin settled into me with a sigh. "I just worry."

"I know you do, but we've trained them well. There's not been a single shift where anything has gone wrong or been forgotten. And if there's a problem, they have our numbers." I leaned in and brushed a kiss along his jaw before nuzzling at his ear. "We have a run, dinner, and kissing in the hot tub to get to."

"Sorry, you lost me at run," Justin said grouchily, but he dropped his head to the side, exposing his neck for my lips.

"The run will make you feel good," I whispered, nipping at the sensitive skin where his neck met his shoulder.

"Kissing in the hot tub would make me feel even better," Justin said.

"Run with me and you can have your hot tub kisses."

"Fine." He sighed. "I'm going to make sure they all know..."

I grabbed him by the waist when he turned for the door. "They know what to do, they've been doing it for nearly three months. Your step-by-step instructions with pictures and flow charts are very descriptive and thorough," I teased. "We're leaving."

Justin pouted. "This is so hard."

"I know. The first time is probably the hardest, but it will get easier." I pulled him close again and rested my forehead against his. "Please. I can't let another job pull me under."

Justin's eyes went wide. "Does this job make you feel like your old one?"

"No, not in the slightest. But I can see us both easily getting sucked under and losing ourselves. We *have* to keep at least a little bit separate—for our sanity." I tipped his chin up and pressed a kiss against his lips. "You know what they say about all work and no play."

Justin stole another kiss. "Fine, fine. I hear you. I'm going out the back because if I go out front, I'll never leave. Meet me at the car?"

"There you go, recognizing your limitations and adjusting. Good job. I'll be there in three minutes or less." I kissed him again, loving that I could, and smiled when he swatted at my ass.

"I'm still voting we skip the run," Justin called out after me.

"Not gonna happen," I said back.

In under three minutes, I climbed into my Jeep, assured Justin everything had been functioning smoothly out front, and headed home.

An hour later, we returned from a particularly difficult run —not because we went on a different path or pushed ourselves farther or faster, but because Justin bitched the entire way. I vowed to make sure we got our morning runs in from that moment on. Justin running after a long day of work and before he had dinner made him hate the activity more than usual.

"See, that wasn't so bad, was it?" I asked as we kicked off our shoes and used our shirts to sop sweat from our brows.

Justin turned his glare my way. "That was absolutely terrible and you know it. Running in the morning is bad enough, but running after all day at work when I'm hungry and missing my baby is torture and I vow to *never* do it again."

"Noted." I did my best to hide my grin. It was actually kind of nice to see Justin grumpy; he was always so enthusiastic about his ideas and the shop, seeing him off his game a bit made him seem more real. "How about you shower while I throw some food together?"

Justin eyed me up and down. "If I wasn't about to drop from the hell you just put me through, I'd ask for a double shower."

"You need food before we do anything else strenuous."

His eyes widened. "How strenuous are we talking because my shower may need an added step."

I chuckled. "I don't think you need to go all out just yet, but we'll be sure to stock up on supplies for future strenuous activities."

Justin narrowed his eyes. "Just to be sure we're on the same page and I'm not inadvertently agreeing to a marathon. I was talking about prepping for sex."

Pulling his damp body close to mine, savoring his scent even when he was covered in sweat, I brushed my lips over his before murmuring in his ear, "So was I."

A shiver traveled through him before he broke away. "Gotcha," he said with a wink as he headed toward the bathroom.

I had all the food prep done by the time Justin emerged from the shower and he took over putting the meal together while I got cleaned up.

When we finally sat down to cilantro lime tilapia with

asparagus and rice, Justin's grumpy mood had lifted and I was a bundle of nerves about hot tub time.

What if what I wanted didn't match what Justin wanted?

What if what I was able to give wasn't good?

What if my imagination had everything hyped up in my head but the reality turned out to be abysmal?

"Get out of your head," Justin said around a bite of fish.

"Huh?" I said, crashing back to the present.

"I don't know what has you frowning and worried, but you need to stop." He gestured toward me with his fork. "Rule number one."

I sighed. "Just kinda worried I've hyped things up between us. Made the hot tub a promise I can't live up to. Imagined things I want to do that I'll be no good at."

"Hey," Justin interrupted as he dropped his fork and came to straddle my lap. "There is no hype, no expectations. The hot tub will feel good on my poor tortured muscles, but nothing has to happen. There's no blueprint here, nothing says we *have* to do anything in particular."

Wrapping my arms around his waist, I pressed a kiss to his chest as I inhaled the fresh, clean scent of laundry detergent on his shirt and body wash on the skin underneath. "And if there are certain things I *really* want to do?"

"We do them," Justin answered with an easy shrug. "I need you to know I'm down for pretty much anything—I mean, I may not be ready for fisting or rolling ourselves in butter while we fuck in public, but…"

I quirked a brow. "Noted."

Justin shrugged. "That night you rubbed my feet was amazing and I'd be good with just that. The things I imagine during my showers are hot as hell and I'd be good with those activities as well. My point being, I just like being with you. Whether we're rubbing feet or rubbing cocks, burning up the sheets or just burning away stress soaking in the hot tub. I don't *need* specific sex acts."

I frowned. "But you like sex, right?"

"I do." He nodded. "But I don't want to come across like we have to do XYZ in order for this new level to be satisfactory for me."

"Okay, that makes sense. As long as it's okay if this new level *does* include XYZ in some variation?" I asked.

"Definitely. I love me some XYZ." Justin rocked his hips against mine and dropped a kiss to my lips.

I growled and gripped his ass. "Are you done eating?"

"Yep," he said, popping the *p*.

"Let's clean this mess up and grab some wine. I hear it's the absolute perfect evening for a soak in the hot tub."

Several minutes later, the kitchen was clean, the dishwasher running, and I carried a large basket tote of items to make our time on the deck more enjoyable.

While I set to work uncovering the tub—glad I'd kept up on the cleaning and checking chemical levels—Justin dug through the basket.

"Such a romantic," he teased as he pulled out three candles.

"More like pragmatic. Those are citronella and there should be another one. Light them and put them around the deck to keep the bugs away." The weather was pleasant, but a recent rain seemed to have multiplied the mosquitos and gnats.

With the candles lit and the water bubbling, I grabbed the wine glasses and bottle of red and placed them at one corner of the sunken hot tub.

"It's pretty private out here, right?" Justin asked as he tossed two towels onto a lounge chair and pulled it close to the steaming water.

"Yeah, why?"

"Can we get in naked?" Justin waggled his brow.

I laughed and stripped my shirt over my head.

Justin's eyes roamed over my body before he licked his lips and pulled his own shirt off. Hooking his thumbs in his sports shorts, he lowered the material slowly, revealing he wore no underwear, and kicked the clothing to the side.

Trying not to swallow my tongue, I took him in. The man was gorgeous. Maybe not in the rock-solid, rippling muscles everywhere perfection type of way, but so damn beautiful I wanted to just reach out and caress every inch of his skin.

Justin ran a hand over his chest down to his plump cock and chuckled nervously. "Feeling a bit underdressed here."

Snapping out of my lust-filled trance, I tore my eyes from Justin's body and quickly slipped my shorts and underwear off, kicking them in the general vicinity of the door.

Thanks to decent genes, I'd never really dealt with much weight gain, but once I hit about forty-five I'd definitely noticed my abs no longer wanted to stay tight and firm. After James died, I'd started running because my doctor told me I wasn't healthy—mainly from stress, but also because I didn't get enough exercise. I knew the daily running I did now kept me in shape and looking good for forty-eight, but I also knew my body was nothing like it had been at Justin's age.

Suddenly *very* self-conscious, I cupped my junk and headed toward the water.

Justin stopped me. "Don't. I just watched a whole scene of self-doubt play out on your face. You're gorgeous. My very own sexy silver fox—hell, I'll call you Daddy if it makes you feel better."

"It doesn't, please don't," I deadpanned.

"Okay, okay." Justin winked and smiled as he wrapped his arms around my neck and brought our bodies together.

The teasing was immediately replaced by the heat of wanting. Every point of contact from our chests to our bellies to our hips, our cocks, our thighs, every place we touched buzzed with hot anticipation.

"My point is," Justin continued, placing open-mouthed kisses along my jaw, "you're hot and sexy and I don't give a damn about your age or if you don't have an eight-pack and biceps the size of my thigh."

I chuckled.

"I only run because you make me. I haven't been to the gym in ages because of all the shop excitement. I sample too many of my own baked goods. I know I *could* look better, but I'm happy with who I am and how I look," Justin said with a shrug.

"You're beautiful," I said. "Don't ever think you're not."

"Same to you. Now, get me in the water before I hump your leg right here." Justin took my hand and followed me to the hot tub.

We stepped down into the water, the top of the tub level with the deck flooring, and both sighed as the hot water bubbled over our tired bodies.

"You're not sitting next to me?" I asked, feeling like a pouty little kid who didn't get to sit next to his friend on the bus.

"Not yet, if I'm too close, too soon, we'll start making out and I'll blow my load in your clean hot tub and all of the magic of the night will swirl away when you drain it to get rid of my spunk." Justin settled on one of the seats across from me and stuck his foot out. "But I'll let you rub my feet."

I laughed as I leaned back in the bucket type seat on my side of the tub and took his foot in my hands. "The chemicals do a pretty good job of keeping the water clean, no worries."

"You jack off in here a lot?" Justin eyed the water suspiciously. "Am I sitting in a bubbling caldron of chlorine and jizz?"

Laughing again—damn, when had I laughed so much? It

felt good to just let go and enjoy myself—I dug my thumbs into the fleshy part of Justin's foot and tried not to focus on how sexy his groan sounded. "No, I save my jacking off for the shower—used to use the bed but it seems rude to rub one out with my husband trying to sleep beside me."

Justin grinned. "Maybe your *husband* could join in one of these days. You know, since we're doing the marital bed shit now and all that."

"Marital bed?" I teased. "Is that what we're doing? Conjugating the marriage?"

Justin just laughed and pulled his foot away. "Next," he said as he slipped his massaged foot between my legs and his other foot into my hands. "Do you ever have Harley and Jo Ellen over to sit in your hot tub?"

"No, we usually just stick to dinner and wine."

"Good, for some reason the thought of simmering in water my grandpa and his girlfriend used kinda squicks me out." Justin shivered, his foot caressing my inner thigh.

"You seem to have a hard time understanding how filtration and chemicals work to keep the water clean," I said with a smirk as I worked my thumbs over the arch of his foot.

Justin shrugged. "Just feels like I'm boiling in a pot. I'd rather not have all their juices bubbling around me."

"My hot tub is clean!" I insisted. "There are no juices."

He moved from his position across from me and came to straddle my hips. "Pretty sure it's going to need cleaned up after tonight. Ouch, this seat is not good for any kind of sexy time," he said as his knees bumped the sides of the bucket seat.

"Let me sit on the bench area." I moved and Justin quickly took his place straddling me again.

"Ah, much better." He leaned in and kissed me, long and slow, our tongues teasing and exploring as his cock pressed against my belly and my hands ran down his back to cup his ass. "Rule number one incoming," he warned. "Can I make a request?"

"We're both rock-hard, hot, and slick in a hot tub and you want to bring up rule number one and requests?" I cocked a brow and pulled him tighter against me, loving the way our bodies fit so perfectly. "I'm clearly already screwing this up." I was teasing, but there was maybe a bit of real doubt buried in there.

"There's definitely nothing wrong with this," Justin assured, rocking his hips, his voice catching slightly. "I just want to ask that you never feel like you have to explain sex to me."

"Huh?" I quirked a grin. "Didn't Harley give you the birds and the bees talk? You know, when two people love each other very much…"

Justin smacked a hand against my chest. "No, not like that you big goof. I'm not making sense." He was flustered.

I moved my hands from his ass and held him, my hands pressed firmly against his back. "Tell me. Rule number one. Always. What's bothering you?"

Justin huffed out a breath. "I know you and James had a different kind of sex life. I just want you to know if you *want* to tell me about it, that's fine. But don't ever think you *have* to explain anything to me. If you want a blow job, ask for a blow job. You don't have to tell me the *why* behind it unless you want to. If you want to top, I'm all for it. You don't have to explain James didn't like certain things. Want to bottom? Same thing, let's do it. I just want you to know I don't *need* an explanation for things you want or things you don't have much experience with. If you want to share all of that, I'm definitely here to listen. I just don't want you to think I'm judging or questioning or need any kind of proof or explanation." He dropped his head to rest against mine. "I don't know if this is making any sense. I guess I mainly just need you to know I respect what you and James had—I know you two were rock-solid and what you had was special. It worked for you. I don't want you to think you have to justify anything to me. What you want to do doesn't need justification. What you haven't had experience with doesn't need justification."

Cupping the back of Justin's neck, I drew him close and whispered, "Thank you," against his lips before deepening the kiss. When we finally broke apart to breathe, I ran a thumb over his lips. "I understand what you're saying and it means a lot. I appreciate you respect what James and I had. It helps to know you're not judging me based on things I haven't done and you're not expecting reasons or explanations, but you're also willing to listen. It may seem simple, but it really helps."

Justin wiggled his ass on my lap, rubbing our cocks together between our bellies. "Can we push rule number one away for a bit and opt for mindless pleasure instead?"

I chuckled. "Let's not get too mindless, I definitely want to be present and know what's going on."

"I have a list a mile long of things we need to do together if I'm to make all of my shower fantasies come true," Justin said with a wink, "but let's start with what you want."

"My list may be just as long, but since we're starting slow…"

Justin scowled. "Now, let's not get carried away. Just because I didn't prep for your dick in my ass doesn't mean we have to proceed like turtles. What's your definition of going slow?"

"Well first, if you keep grinding our dicks together, it's not going to matter because I'm going to blow before we get to anything else." I gripped his hips and slowed his movements.

Justin grinned. "We're already naked so I'm guessing you're not insinuating we just dry hump each other like teens. I'm fine with hand jobs if that's where you want to start, but…"

I winced. "Gotta be honest, I've done my own hand jobs for so long—and don't get me wrong, I'm sure your hand would feel amazing—I'm really wanting something a bit more."

"Tell me what you want," Justin murmured against my lips. "I wanna hear you say it."

I knew what I wanted and I knew Justin didn't need or expect an explanation. "I wanna taste you," I said. "Wanna feel the weight of your cock on my tongue, your cock head pressing the back of my throat." James had occasionally sucked me off because he knew I liked it, but he was repulsed by receiving oral sex.

"Whoa, cowboy, let's not get too carried away. My dick is average, not the massive meat-stick most porn would have you believe is real. Bumping the back of your throat is a goal, not a guarantee," Justin teased, relieving most of my nervous anticipation.

"I can deal with that. While we're at it, let's remember not everyone is gifted at sucking dick and I may be terrible at it." I reached between us and took our shafts in hand.

"Hot wet lips and tongue on my cock? Keep the teeth away and there couldn't be anything terrible about it." Justin glanced over his shoulder. "Go back to that low seat."

Having no idea what he planned to do, I moved to settle into the bucket seat which put me low enough the water was over my shoulders.

Justin stood in front of me straddling my legs, his cock bobbing proudly right in front of my face.

Pushing aside insecurities, I cupped his balls as the water bubbled around his legs. Caressing the warm skin of his inner thigh, coarse hair under my palm, I made my way to his dick. Gripping the base, I leaned in and licked a trail from root to tip, loving the smooth skin under my tongue. Justin's flavor, made up of skin, soap, chlorine, and the bitter saltiness of his pre-cum, filled my mouth and I yearned for more than just a taste.

Justin groaned and reached to clasp his hand over my fist already gripping his dick. "Suck me," he said, half plea, half demand.

I swirled my tongue around his leaking head before opening my mouth. I reveled in the stretch of my lips around his thickness as Justin slowly fed me his cock. The slick weight of his wet, satiny skin on my tongue went straight to my already throbbing dick and I bobbed my head, his shaft sliding in and out of my mouth. Wanting more, wanting to feel Justin explode on my tongue, I reached for his hips and pulled him closer, nearly gagging as his balls rubbed my chin and his cock head brushed the back of my throat.

Justin moaned and leaned forward, resting his hands on the side of the hot tub as I sank back in the low seat. The shift in our position allowed me to look up at Justin's face as he thrust his hips, pumping his cock in and out of my greedy mouth.

He stared down at me, a look of awe and complete bliss filling his face. "Fuck, Morgan," he said, panting. "Fuck, that's good."

His words filled me with pride and spurred me on. I gripped his ass, holding tight as he fucked into me. Moving one hand to his tight balls, I moaned around his cock as I teased a finger against his taint.

Justin's thrusting faltered when my finger slipped between his ass cheeks and brushed over his hole. Not wanting to take my mouth from his cock, I glanced up at him questioningly, my finger poised to either retreat or forge on.

He nodded. "You can touch me," he said. "Please."

Allowing all the filthy fantasies I'd had about Justin to dance happily through my head, I let my wet finger push and tease against his tight pucker as he continued to fuck my face. With each press of my finger, Justin grunted and groaned. When I finally worked him open enough to slide my finger inside, he froze.

"Fuck," he said, huffing. "Don't stop. Just give me a second or I'm gonna blow."

I nodded my head—encouraging him to let loose— gripping his hip in one hand and slipping my finger deeper into his tight ass.

Justin stuttered a breathy laugh mixed with another moan. "As long as I get to suck you next."

In answer, I flattened my tongue against his shaft and brushed my finger against what I assumed—okay, more like *hoped*—was his prostate. When Justin gasped and bucked his hips, I figured I'd hit the right spot.

"I'm gonna come," Justin warned, as if that wasn't exactly what I was waiting for.

I fingered his hole and did my best to swallow him down —definitely needed practice to decrease my gag reflex—and hummed around his shaft.

Justin tensed and groaned as his ass clenched around my finger and his cock pulsed, shooting hot, salty spurts onto my tongue. Swallowing all I could, not even minding as some dribbled from the corner of my mouth, I eased my finger from his ass and stood to wrap my arms around his quivering body. As steam rose from my warm, wet skin, I walked him to the other side of the tub, my rock-hard cock throbbing and begging between us.

Justin turned us as he gripped the back of my neck and devoured my mouth, licking his cum from my chin before diving into my mouth as if savoring his flavor on my tongue.

The night air was pleasant as it cooled my skin. Justin reached for a towel from the lounge chair and spread it on the deck. "Sit on the edge, lean back on your hands," he ordered.

I followed the request, shivering slightly as a breeze tickled over my damp skin. Sitting on the edge of the tub, leaning back on my hands, my throbbing cock stood proudly from a trimmed thatch of silver and black hair.

"This okay?" Justin asked as he knelt on the bench seat between my spread legs and bent to nuzzle his nose at the junction of my leg.

"Yeah, it's good," I said, giving my balls a squeeze in hopes of staving off anything trying to happen way too quickly.

Justin bent slightly and hefted my legs over his shoulders before leaning in to press kisses against my fingers just before he removed them from my balls. Caressing his tongue against my tight sac, he gripped my cock and stroked slowly. "Been thinking about sucking you off for months," he said before licking my head and teasing his tongue into my slit.

With a moan, I dropped from my hands to my elbows, remaining propped up so I could see everything Justin was doing. As my heart filled my chest to nearly-bursting and Justin's eyes caught mine, I watched him spread my pre-cum against his lips just before he opened his mouth and took me in. The wet heat surrounding my shaft was a stark contrast to the cool air drying my skin and the opposite sensations sent shivers through me.

He sucked and licked while stroking my base with one hand and teasing a finger from taint to hole making me groan and fist the towel. "Still okay?" Justin asked.

"God, yes," I answered, dropping my head back to savor the sensation of his mouth on my dick and his finger pressing against my entrance. But I couldn't stand not watching, so I lifted my head again, unable to take my eyes off of Justin's mouth stretched around my cock.

"Wanna taste your cum on my tongue," Justin said when he popped off my dick. "Want you to come for me."

"Don't want it to be over too soon." I thrust my hips up, my wet cock sliding through his fist.

"We've got time." Justin licked my balls. "So much I wanna do with you."

"Tell me."

"Gonna rim you until you're begging and then slide my dick deep into your ass," Justin murmured, nuzzling his nose against the base of my cock. "Wanna feel your cock buried in my ass. Gonna fuck you and fill you with my cum. Then you'll spread me open and pump me full of your cum while mine is dripping from your hole."

His dirty promises and the way he took me deep into his mouth again, coupled with his wet finger breaching my tight pucker and sliding deep, was all it took to send me over the edge. My release washed over me as I unloaded on Justin's tongue, my ass gripping his finger over and over as my cock pulsed in his mouth.

"Fuck," I groaned, panting as the last of my orgasm coursed through me. "Come here." I reached for Justin, wincing slightly as he pulled from my ass and let my softening cock slip from his mouth. Loving the way Justin's warm, wet body straddled mine as he leaned down to bring us chest-to-chest, I wrapped my arms around his back and pulled him in for a deep, searching kiss. The taste of myself on his tongue mixed with the remnants of Justin on mine, and made for an intoxicating flavor that had my spent cock valiantly attempting a comeback.

"You good?" Justin asked, cupping my cheek and brushing a thumb over my lips.

I grunted in response and ran my hands down his back to

grip his ass just as a strong breeze swept over our bodies. "Shit, that's a little too cold. You wanna get back in the water or go inside?"

Justin shivered. "Inside. You've exhausted me."

I chuckled and slapped his ass.

We made quick work of gathering everything and covering the tub before making our way inside.

"We didn't drink our wine, you want some?" I asked.

"Yeah, let's veg out on the couch with wine," Justin said as he pulled on his shorts.

I poured the wine and pulled on my own shorts. "Lead the way so that we may *veg*," I teased.

Justin grabbed the remote and flopped down onto the couch. I handed him his wine and set the half empty bottle on the coffee table before sinking down next to him.

We sipped our wine for a few quiet moments as Justin flipped through the guide looking for something to watch.

"Are we okay?" Justin blurted.

I turned to face him. "I'm good. You?"

He nodded. "Yeah, that was amazing."

"So, what are you worried about?"

Justin shrugged. "Just don't want sex to ruin what we had. Seems like most guys I've ever had sex with got tired of me once they got me into bed." He huffed. "Or once they stole my money and took off."

I put my arm around him, pulled him close, and kissed the top of his head. "We're better than that. I'm definitely not tired of you. Plus, we have too much going on to get tired of each other." Tipping his chin to make his eyes meet mine, I brushed a kiss against his lips. "If you don't *want* to take things further than we did tonight, no worries. It stops here. But if you're still on board, I'm definitely on the same page."

Justin nodded. "I'm on board."

I cleared my throat. "Did you mean all that stuff you said or was that just heat-of-the-moment dirty talk?"

Justin grinned and narrowed his eyes. "Why? Did the thought of my tongue in your ass get you hot? Thinking about fucking me while my cum dripped from your hole turned you on?"

I groaned, draining the rest of my wine in one gulp and adjusting my resurrecting cock. "Not gonna lie, yeah, you got my fantasies swirling double-time."

"Hope wherever you're taking me this weekend has privacy or really good sound-proofing," Justin teased.

I raised a brow.

"We have a lot of making fantasies come true to do." Justin swallowed the rest of his wine and leaned in to kiss me. "Until then, maybe we take this little party to the bedroom? I'm thinking I'd like to rub off on my husband's cock before I crash."

I growled as I stood and yanked him to his feet. "Always love your ideas," I said as I stroked my ready and willing cock.

That's how I found myself naked between Justin's spread legs as we rocked our leaking cocks together. He whispered dirty words in my ear, making me picture all the things he promised we'd do, and we ended up shooting our loads between us as I stroked our cocks to completion.

After a quick clean-up, I wrapped Justin in my arms and we slept like the dead until my alarm went off the next morning.

THIRTEEN
JUSTIN

I KNEW Morgan hadn't had a lot of experience with giving head since James wasn't a fan and I'd be damned if I was going to complain about waking up to his perfect lips wrapped around my dick.

"Fuck," I murmured as I woke to the wet heat of his mouth. "*Good* morning to me."

Morgan chuckled around me and I moaned at the vibration.

Assuming he wasn't well-practiced in the sixty-nine position, I quickly rearranged our bodies and took his heavy shaft in my hand. "First one to get off makes breakfast." I wasn't sure if that was a prize or a consequence and I didn't even care.

Morgan groaned, his nose nuzzling the trimmed pubes at the base of my cock, and sucked harder as I tongued his slit before sinking my mouth down his length.

I counted myself a winner when my balls drew up tight and I unloaded on Morgan's tongue just as his cock pulsed and spurted thick and hot onto mine. Popping off his spent shaft, I moved to bring our mouths level with each other and kissed him deeply, spreading our flavors between us.

"Thought you were worried about dragon breath in the morning?" Morgan teased against my lips.

"Figured the taste of cock and cum would overpower morning breath," I said, pressing a final kiss to his mouth. "Plus, I woke up with my dick buried in your mouth, I wasn't exactly thinking clearly. Now, I get to make breakfast while you shower. We aren't in a huge hurry, but we can't dawdle."

"Nice try," Morgan said. "We run first."

I growled and flopped onto the bed. "I don't wanna."

"We run, then showers and breakfast before heading to the big celebration. We have time and you know you'll feel so much better the rest of the day." Morgan pulled me to stand and kissed me again. "Plus, we may not have the chance to run while we're gone, so we don't want to skip today."

"Oh, I'm fine with skipping today. I assure you." But I got dressed and followed him to the door. With my running shoes laced up, I grumbled, "I want it noted how much I despise this."

"I know you do. And that's why I appreciate having you with me even more." Morgan smacked my ass. "Let's go."

As much as I hated it—and hated admitting it even more —the run did wonders for my head and body and, by the time we got to Piping Hot, I was on top of the world.

Morgan, Jo Ellen, Harley, and I spent the next several hours chatting with our regulars and those who mostly just came in for freebies. We gave away samples, loyalty cards, and prizes like they were candy. Every single thing we put in customer hands either had our name and logo on it or came with a loyalty card that already had a few of our signature flame punches on it. The day was meant for celebrating the new shop and our recent changes and successes, but Morgan and I had agreed it was a good day for marketing as well.

We'd give regulars reason to return and hopefully hook some newbies.

The entire day had me floating on cloud nine. Not only were we showing off our superb coffee, tea, baked goods, and food while visiting with our friends and customers, something had definitely changed between Morgan and me.

Up until that moment, we'd touch and kiss in public just to make things look real and believable. But now, there were brushes of fingers, longing gazes, winks and smiles, stolen kisses, and hip bumps that had nothing to do with putting on a show and I absolutely loved it.

Would it make the end of our year all that much more difficult? For sure. Was it worth it? I thought about the spectacular sex we'd had the night before, the sensual wake-up we'd shared that morning, and the way Morgan smiled at me when he wrapped his arm around me to brag about the changes I'd brought to Piping Hot. Yeah, getting to experience this with Morgan was worth any heartache later on.

Or at least that's what I'd keep telling myself because there was no way I could give up what Morgan and I had started the night before. Maybe I'd regret it at the end of our year, but I had no regrets right then.

As the celebration wound down, Jo beamed at us over the table she was washing. "Marriage and settling into the business looks good on you two." She cocked her head. "Maybe it was the stress in the beginning, but you look like you've finally found your stride." She continued with a fond smile. "No one ever really understood what Ron and I had—our age gap was twenty-five years and most just thought he was preying on me. But I was a headstrong eighteen-year-old when I met him and I knew from the very first moment he was the man I wanted to spend my life with. We were a strong force to be reckoned with and we did a lot of good during the time we were given. Don't ever let anyone make you feel your age difference is a negative. You two are good together and I don't want you to ever forget that."

I smirked at Morgan who just smiled and shook his head.

Later, in the kitchen, Grandpa Harley patted my shoulder as he dropped off an empty tray. "Cookies were a big hit."

"Everyone loves cookies," I said, washing a mixing bowl.

"You've done a really great thing here. I'm proud of you."

"Thanks." My heart caught in my throat. After always being the reject and the odd-man-out with my parents and siblings, it was nice to hear some praise. Harley had always been proud of me, but it still felt good to hear it.

"I'm sorry I questioned you and Morgan back in the beginning," Harley said. "I was wrong, you two seem really happy together. I should have known better than to judge—hell, Jo and I are probably the least likely perfect match in the world, but we make it work because we work *together*. So, I had no right to say if you and Morgan got together too quickly or made hasty decisions."

My gut churned with guilt. I wanted to tell Harley the truth. He was my grandpa and he loved me unconditionally. But he was too connected to Jo Ellen and I wouldn't ask him to keep things from her, so I kept my mouth shut. What Morgan and I started with had morphed into something we hadn't planned on. No reason to bring others in on it when what we had *now* was far removed from the farce at the very beginning. "Thanks. We are happy. He's a good man and a good business partner."

Morgan walked into the kitchen and immediately picked up a towel to help with drying some of the dishes. After chatting with Harley as we finished the task, Morgan snapped the towel at my ass and laughed when I yelped.

"You ready?" Morgan asked.

"We're leaving now?"

"Yep, the shifts are all covered—even made sure we have some extras on-call as needed—and the crew doesn't expect to see us back until Monday. We're going home to pack and heading out."

Harley raised a brow. "Where are you going?"

"I don't know, he won't tell me." I scowled. "All I know is he's taking me away from my baby."

Morgan smiled and wrapped an arm around my shoulders, pressing a kiss against my temple. "What I'm doing is making sure we don't get burned out *and* providing us with that honeymoon we were too swamped to take a few months ago."

I huffed, but tossed the wet towels in a laundry bin and took off my apron. Jo Ellen had been aghast we weren't taking a honeymoon after the wedding so using this little weekend getaway to appease her—even if it was really just for us—worked in our advantage. But I didn't like not knowing where we were going.

"Well, have fun and be careful," Harley said. "We'll help keep an eye on things here."

An hour later, our bags were packed and we hit the road. Morgan pointed the Jeep toward the state line and told me to turn on some music.

"Are you going to tell me where we're going?" I grumbled as I set a playlist to play low over the speakers.

"No, it's a surprise and you'll love it. I promise." Morgan reached for my hand and gave it a squeeze. "I wouldn't take you somewhere you'd be miserable."

The warm late afternoon sun on my face and Morgan's hand on mine mixed with the music and the motion of the Jeep to lull me to sleep. When Morgan gently jostled me awake, I woke with a start and checked the time. I'd been asleep for two hours.

"You let me sleep the whole way?" I ran a hand over my face.

"You needed it," Morgan said with a shrug. "Plus, this way, it's *really* a surprise because you didn't see where we were going."

I glanced around at the sun-dappled wooded area where the Jeep sat. "And exactly where did we go?"

"We've got a private cabin, no one around, a lake, hiking trails, a sauna and hot tub, chef-prepared ready-to-bake meals, a double-headed shower, and a king-sized bed all at our disposal for the next couple days." Morgan gestured out the window and I caught sight of the massive cabin—okay, more like *mansion*—nestled back from the driveway.

"Oh my God, it's gorgeous. How did you find this place? Who owns it?" I climbed from the Jeep and stretched, breathing in deeply as the fresh air and the early evening sunshine washed over me.

"I found it by asking around. Right now, an older couple owns it and rents it out. We only lucked out to get it on short notice because the people who rented it for this weekend ended up with a kid having appendicitis." Morgan grabbed our bags and jingled keys in his hands. "Wanna see inside?"

We made our way into the massive cabin and I truly hadn't ever seen anything so beautiful. "Whoa, this is impressive." I stood in the middle of the vast, open living room and turned around slowly, taking in the amazing view. "Maybe one day I'll be successful enough to own something like this and prove to my family I've *made it*."

Morgan frowned. "Is owning something like this what you'd want?"

I shrugged. "My parents and siblings would own it just for status. They'd look at this place as their idea of roughing it and brag about it to their friends. I'd want to own it as a private getaway and a reminder to rest and relax. I know I don't have to prove anything to them. I guess I just wish someday they'd actually be proud of me or think I've made something of myself."

Morgan wrapped his arms around my waist and pulled me in for a slow, deep kiss. "I get it, but I also need you to know you don't need their approval. You are a smart, savvy, successful businessman. Period. They may never see you that way—honestly, I've never met them, but I sometimes wonder if maybe they're jealous of the easy, simple life you've chosen and the fact you've still had so much success—but *I* see you that way. Harley and Jo see you that way. The whole town of Briarton sees you that way. You *have* made it, whether that part of your family ever acknowledges it or not. Their definition of *making it* isn't the only right one."

My eyes stung with unshed tears and I buried my face in Morgan's neck. "Thank you. I've never had my very own cheerleader aside from Harley and it's kinda nice."

"I'll be your hype man any day. Now, let's unpack and check out this place."

The cabin was nestled snuggly among hills, a lake, and a burbling brook. The views were absolutely stunning and I made Morgan promise we'd eat on the deck overlooking the fabulous view for each meal.

The hot tub on the deck gave me all kinds of sexy thoughts, but the sauna in the basement also had me making plans. The king-sized bed was similar to ours back home, but the mirrored closets were a definite difference.

"The décor is outdated and kinda cringy," I said as I eyed the mirrors. "But I can definitely see the appeal of mirrors in the bedroom."

Morgan chuckled. "You have plans? Thinking there may be activity you'd like to watch?"

My cock twitched as a flame glowed hot in my gut. "I think I can't wait to watch us together on this bed. Don't get me wrong, I wanna get sexy in the hot tub and the sauna as well. Maybe even on a hiking trail. Definitely in the double shower. But the main attraction is gonna be right here where we can be our very own audience."

Morgan groaned and pushed me to the bed, nestling his hips between my spread legs and devouring my mouth. "Let's check what our meal situation is, chill some wine, and take a walk first. Then we can make all of those plans happen."

I wrapped my legs around his waist. "It's nearly dark now. Let's get off so I'm not rock-hard during dinner. Save the walk for tomorrow. Dinner, sauna, showers, then the big show here with these gaudy mirrors."

Morgan eagerly obliged by stripping us to bare skin and rocking our cocks together as our tongues fucked into each other's mouths until we shot our thick, hot loads between us.

After a quick clean-up and donning only underwear, Morgan and I made our way to the kitchen to see what our meal options were.

"How did you set up meals like this?" I asked as we peered into the refrigerator at six neatly packaged meal kits.

Morgan shrugged. "I asked the couple who rent it out about meal options and they said we could bring groceries *or* put in an order with them and they'd have meals here ready to prepare. I thought the meals could be fun and the extra expense would save us on groceries and time."

We opted for cedar plank salmon, Brussels sprouts, garlic mashed potatoes, and miniature Bundt cakes for dessert. The food was spectacular and had my baker brain going a million miles a minute.

"We definitely need to either figure out where this food was ordered from or practice that meal on our own at home. Delicious." I rinsed the sink as we finished clean up. "But the

Bundt cakes are for sure going into rotation at the shop. I'm thinking we add our own little flair to them. Mix it up with flavors. Do the traditional flavors like vanilla, chocolate, lemon, and cinnamon, but also add in unique flavors with glazes and icing. Like chocolate with an orange glaze, lemon with a lavender icing, vanilla with a mocha icing." I made some quick notes on my phone. "I'm going to do some practice runs with mini Bundt cakes—I'm thinking we can have little bite-sized ones and maybe one size larger, about the size of our cinnamon rolls—then we'll get them in front of the customers and see how they do. If they're a hit, we add them to the menu rotation."

Morgan smiled and shook his head as he pulled me close and tipped up my chin with his finger. "I love the way your brain works." He lowered his head and brushed a kiss over my lips.

Losing all interest in any dessert other than the man kissing me, I tossed my phone on the kitchen counter and deepened the kiss. A thousand thoughts bounced in my mind as our warm, slick tongues mated and Morgan held me tighter—how lucky I was to have him in my life, how much I adored running a business with him, how grateful I was he took me away for a break.

But mostly the fact I was pretty sure I'd gone and fallen in love with him and how much I never wanted what we had to end

I wanted to tear up every calendar, stomp my feet, and declare our one-year deal a huge mistake. More than anything, I longed for Morgan to tell me he felt the same.

But I was being selfish. I'd been granted a lot more than I deserved when I met him and yanked him into my life. I'd been blessed to receive six months longer than originally planned. I wouldn't be greedy and ask for more.

But it wouldn't stop me from wishing and hoping every

single day that *maybe* Morgan would eventually want more with me.

"Let's try that sauna," I murmured against Morgan's lips.

We made our way to the basement and turned on the sauna. As we stripped out of our underwear, gathered towels, and sprinkled water over the hot rocks, steam filled the air in the small space.

"This is nice," I said. "Not sure how practical it would be —like is a sauna something I'd sit in every day? But it's nice." I settled in on the bench as the steamy warmth enveloped me.

"I can see it being really nice after a long run," Morgan said. "Honestly, I've looked at the infrared saunas as an option. I wouldn't have room inside the apartment—well, I *would*, but I'm not sure I want a big-ass sauna in my living room. But I could put it on the deck."

"What's the difference? Infrared versus this one?"

"Benefits seem to be similar," Morgan said. "Better sleep, relaxation, detoxification, relief from muscle and joint pain, are some of the big ones. Just different ways of heating and supposedly the infrared heat is more directly on the body rather than the surrounding air."

I moaned as the warm air relaxed my whole body. "I'd think it's more of a dry heat than this steamy heat?"

"Yeah, I think so. I may look into getting one for the deck. We could relax after a long day."

I loved that Morgan included me in his plans, but I wondered if he, too, constantly thought about that end date. Sure, it was still a bit away, but it loomed over me and never left my mind.

After twenty minutes, the sauna shut off.

"I don't want to move," I mumbled.

"How about if we move just to the shower?" Morgan stood and pulled me to my feet.

As we climbed the stairs and made our way to the bedroom, I let my warm, smooshy brain mull over the next couple hours. "Hey, not to interrupt our total Zen state, but what are your thoughts on tonight's activities?"

Morgan cocked a brow.

My cheeks heated and I ducked my head. "Like what *types* of activities are we thinking? The answer changes our shower situation."

Realization dawned on Morgan's face and he stuttered, "Oh, um, how about we split up our showers and meet in the big double one when we're both a little more prepared?"

"Perfect. I'll take the second-floor bathroom. Give me about thirty minutes."

Morgan kissed me. "I'll use the hallway bathroom on this floor. Meet you in the ensuite in a bit."

We each took our bags from the bedroom and made our way to our separate bathrooms. Glad I'd thrown prep materials into my overnight bag, I flipped on a playlist and took care of essentials as I eagerly anticipated what I expected to be magnificent sex.

Thirty minutes later, I wandered into the big bathroom to find Morgan turning on the water. The double shower heads rained down and he adjusted them so we could stand right in the middle and get showered from both sides.

"This is really nice," I said as I stepped into the shower and closed the glass door behind me. "Our place doesn't have the room for *this* big of a shower, but I wonder if we could swing at least the double heads."

Morgan wrapped his arms around my waist and pressed our dicks together. "Speaking of double heads," he murmured against my lips and then groaned. "Oh my God, sorry. That was cheesy and so, so bad."

I chuckled. "I don't mind. Seems my brain pretty much short-circuits anytime I'm naked around you."

Morgan smiled. "Obviously, mine does too if I'm saying stupid stuff like that."

"What do you want to do in here?" I ran my hands down his back, gripping his ass and pulling our hips together. "I'm not against shower sex, but I will tell you it's not *as* great as fictional settings would have you believe. Maybe we save anything involving dicks in asses for the bedroom."

"Sounds good to me." Morgan kissed up my neck before biting my earlobe, sending desire shooting straight to my cock. "How do you feel about cocks in mouths and fingers in asses for shower time?"

"I love the way your brain works," I tossed his words back to him as I pressed kisses along his jaw, his neck, and his collar bone. Pausing to tease his nipples, flicking them with my tongue and nibbling softly, I smiled at Morgan's groan. He shifted to lean against the tiled wall as I dropped to my knees and stroked his cock. Swirling my tongue around his head, savoring the salty burst of flavor from his pre-cum, I used one hand to cup his balls and one hand to run my slick fingers between his perfect ass cheeks as I took his length between my lips.

"Shit," Morgan panted as he dropped his head against the wall. "Fuck, that's good." He widened his stance and placed his hand on my head as I took him deep while fondling his balls.

When I slicked my finger with spit, Morgan gripped my head a bit tighter. As I worked my finger against his hole and began to press at the tight pucker, he thrust his hips harder. Moving my hand from his sac to grip his ass, I increased the speed of my mouth on his dick and teased my finger deeper into him, loving the way Morgan shivered and moaned my name.

"Give me more," he demanded, his hands fisting in my hair.

"No lube, might sting," I warned.

Morgan bucked his hips. "I want it. Wanna feel it. Not gonna last much longer."

I slowly worked a second finger into him, breaching the tight muscle as Morgan tensed slightly. "You okay?" I asked.

"Yeah, it stings, but it's good. Suck me," Morgan begged.

With my fist around his shaft and two fingers in his ass, I pumped his cock as I sucked him deep. My own cock bobbed hard and heavy, aching for attention and relief.

Morgan thrust hard and fast, his fingers weaved through my hair as he fucked my face. "Fuck, I'm gonna come. Fuck." His throbbing cock pulsed between my lips, his salty bitterness unloading on my tongue. As a final shiver traveled through Morgan's body, I slipped my fingers from his tight ass and allowed him to pull me to my feet.

His lips descended on mine and I welcomed his tongue into my mouth with an eager moan. When we broke apart to breathe, Morgan tipped my chin as he stroked my aching cock. "Can we get in bed? Want you to straddle me and let me suck you off."

I gripped my balls, praying his words alone wouldn't have me blowing my load. "Fuck, yeah."

Morgan quickly turned off the water and we half-assed dried ourselves before we rushed to the bed. Morgan flipped on a lamp as I turned off the overhead light. The large uncovered picture window facing the woods reflected our naked bodies as we crawled onto the mattress—not gonna lie, the thought of anyone on the outside watching us while we watched ourselves in the mirrored closet was a complete and total turn-on.

Once Morgan tossed lube on the bed and positioned himself on his back, I straddled his chest, my tight balls pressed against his damp skin. I glanced toward our dark reflection in the window and shivered before gazing at the mirrors.

Morgan caught where my eyes had landed and he gripped my thighs. "We look pretty damn gorgeous together."

I moaned and rocked my hips, loving the way his fingers bit into my skin. "So hot. Gonna watch while you suck me off."

Morgan's tongue flicked out to lick my leaking cock head as he pulled me closer. "Give it to me," he demanded. "Don't stop until you're shooting down my throat."

"Pretty sure that's going to be in about five seconds, so if you're wanting to get those fingers in my ass, I suggest you lube up and get in there." I waited a moment for Morgan to slick lube on his fingers and around my hole before I pressed my throbbing dick against his lips. Whimpering at the sight of my cock sliding into his waiting mouth, I turned toward the mirrors and nearly blew my load right then and there.

Morgan pressed his slick finger against my tight pucker and I welcomed the stretch as he slid in deep. "Fuck, give me another one. Wanna feel you in me when I come."

The sting of Morgan's second finger made me catch my breath, but I gripped the headboard and rode his fingers as my cock thrust in and out of his mouth. When Morgan shifted his position slightly and brushed over that sweet spot deep inside, I groaned on a final thrust as my orgasm washed over me, my cock pulsing thick and hot onto Morgan's tongue, my ass clenching on his fingers.

When I came back to earth, Morgan slid from my body and wrapped me in his arms as he devoured my mouth, teasing and exploring, tasting and savoring. "That was fucking amazing," he said when we broke apart.

"It was. Sleep and see if we're up for anything later?"

Morgan agreed sleep was a good idea and grabbed a wet cloth for a quick clean-up. As he gathered me in his arms, I did my best to push away the thoughts of how hard I'd fallen for him and how badly I wanted to beg that it never had to end.

An hour or so later, I woke to soft kisses against my neck and a rock-hard cock against my ass. I rocked into Morgan and groaned as his hand came around to stroke my cock. "Wanna be inside you," he whispered gruffly against my ear.

"We haven't talked about condoms," I answered, wanting nothing more than for him to slick his dick and slide into me.

"I brought some if you want them. I've had routine testing every year since James and I were together and since he passed. Negative results."

"I've had as many tests as feasibly possible ever since Sean ran off and I realized he probably had other guys on the side. I'm negative."

"It's your call. I'm good with either way. Don't want you to feel pressured one way or another," Morgan said, tipping my chin so I was looking right into his eyes.

"Without. Wanna feel all of you," I said. Possibly the dumbest decision I'd made since Sean. Not because I worried for my health or safety, I knew Morgan would never purposely put me at risk. But sex with the man I'd have to give up in less than a year was already doing wickedly terrible things to my heart. Feeling him bare inside me, allowing that level of intimacy I didn't even allow with Sean over two years, was for sure going to tear me apart.

"What position works for you?" Morgan asked as he grabbed the lube and slicked his shaft.

"Wanna be on my back so I can see the mirrors," I answered with zero hesitation.

"Who knew I had myself a little voyeur?" Morgan teased as I rolled to my back and spread my legs for him. He coated my hole with lube and teased a finger inside before pressing my legs farther apart and tapping the head of his cock against my entrance.

Torn between watching us in the mirror and watching Morgan's face as he entered me, I kept my eyes on his as he breached my tight muscle. "Oh fuck," I panted, all breath leaving me as he stretched me open and the feeling of absolutely-perfect-in-every-way washed over me.

Morgan knelt between my legs and paused for a moment as he gripped my leg and lifted it to his shoulder, kissing my ankle, my calf, my knee. "You good?" he asked.

Turning my head to catch sight of us in the mirrors, I nodded as I stroked my cock. "Mmm, yeah."

Morgan thrust into me, his cock sliding in and out of my tight, sensitive hole as we watched the show. Pre-cum leaked onto my belly, my soft whimpers filling the air. When Morgan shifted his position, leaning forward to bring us chest-to-chest and gripping my chin to make me meet his eyes, I lost all interest in the mirror; I only had eyes for the man on top of me, holding me, pumping his cock into me. "Want your eyes on me when I come in you," Morgan said, his gruff words sending an electric shock straight to my dick.

"Do it, wanna feel it, please," I begged as Morgan wrapped me in his arms, increasing the speed and strength of his thrusts. With my legs tangled around his waist and my hands gripping his shoulders, I held on for the ride.

"Jack yourself, wanna watch you come with me," Morgan demanded.

Reaching between us, my cock already close to exploding from the friction of our abdomens as Morgan fucked me, I gripped my shaft and stroked. "Fuck, fuck," I panted, "gonna come."

As an orgasm shuddered through me, my cock pulsing my release between us and my ass clenching Morgan's dick, he gave a final thrust and shot his load deep into me. "Holy shit," Morgan bit out as he dropped his forehead to mine and kissed me. "Haven't done that in ages, and only once before." He pulled back to look into my eyes. "Was it okay?"

Cupping his cheek, I pulled him close to kiss him again. "It was amazing." In all actuality, it was probably the best sex I'd ever had—likely due to the emotional connection I so easily felt with Morgan—but I wasn't sure admitting that was the best thing to do when your marriage was a temporary thing.

As we caught our breaths, Morgan chuckled. "I can't stop thinking about what you said about fucking me and then me fucking you as your cum drips from my ass."

I laughed. "I've created a monster."

"You really think you could come in me without me getting off and then flip so I could fuck you? I know some men are super sensitive after they come."

I shrugged. "I think I could. If not, you could jack off on me while I dripped from your ass."

"Always so full of great ideas," Morgan teased, brushing his lips along my jaw before kissing me softly.

Clenching my ass around his softening cock, I bit my lip. "Full of ideas is good. Full of your cock is better."

Morgan groaned as he slipped from my body and grabbed the cloth we'd used earlier for a quick clean-up. "We should sleep. I wanna get up for a sunrise hike tomorrow."

"As long as *hike* doesn't turn into *run*, I'm game. Think there's a boat to go out on the lake?" I cuddled into Morgan's arms as he pulled the blanket up around our shoulders.

"I'd say there probably is. We can shower, eat breakfast, and check before we start our hike." He kissed me on top of my head as I drifted to sleep.

FOURTEEN

MORGAN

OUR WEEKEND away was absolutely perfect with the exception of the time passing too quickly. I was already making plans to book another weekend at the cabin. If I was being honest, I wanted to make the cabin our own personal sanctuary to where I'd whisk Justin every time we needed a break or a reconnection.

But reconnecting was for couples who needed to keep their relationship together and Justin and I had no need for that. Despite how badly I wanted to grip his shoulders, shake him, and beg for him to let this thing between us play out naturally rather than ending in a year, I kept telling myself it was selfish and unfair.

So, I enjoyed every single second of our weekend and did my best to commit everything about Justin to memory to savor and reminisce over in the lonely days ahead of me.

We took a canoe out on the lake and I laughed my ass off when Justin accidentally tipped us over trying to get a better look at a turtle. He didn't find it as funny.

The sauna and hot tub were wondrous for our exhausted muscles after we took several hikes. I never wanted to forget the way the sunlight glinted on Justin's brown hair and dappled the floor of the wooded area where I dropped to my knees and took him in my mouth. I teased him that his whimpering moans had scared away the wildlife, but just the memory of the way he gripped my head and unloaded on my tongue was enough to get me hard again, wildlife be damned.

When Justin had suggested we spend one more night at the cabin and leave extra early to head back to Briarton, a strange warmth had washed over me. Knowing he'd enjoyed our time together as much as I had—knowing we were both too worn out and sore for anything sexual and happily agreed to just cuddling on the couch on our last night—gave me a ridiculous surge of hope that maybe Justin felt something more than temporary for me as well.

What I'd *do* with that hope, I wasn't sure. But it definitely did funny things to my insides.

After I loaded the Jeep in the dark predawn hours, I made coffee and took mine to the deck to wait for Justin to finish in the shower. In the secluded quiet, my thoughts roared. Thoughts of James, what our future would have been like had he not died, what he would have thought of Briarton, Piping Hot, this cabin. But if James hadn't died, I wouldn't have the things lighting such a fire in my soul.

Did James have to die for me to be happy? How fucked up was that? I was happy with him—I loved him with every ounce of my being. Never wanted anything different or more. But there I was, enjoying my new home, my new job, my *new husband*, and a happiness I wasn't sure I'd ever known, and the only way any of that came to be was because my best friend died. What a punch to the gut.

And the most painful hit of all?

I'd gone and fallen head-over-heels in love with Justin.

Was I betraying James?

Did falling for Justin and feeling things so differently

between us mean what I'd had with James wasn't real and good?

"You seem deep in thought," Justin said as he wrapped an arm around my waist.

I grunted.

"Rule number one?"

I sighed. "Distracted. Lots of thoughts and feelings."

"Wanna tell me about them?" Justin hedged.

Chuckling before taking a sip of coffee, I gazed around the wooded area just as a pink glow began to rise from the horizon. "Mind's a bit chaotic right now. Thinking about how James wouldn't have liked this place, but he would have suffered through for me. Feeling guilty I love my new home and my new job—guilty I had such a great time with you this weekend." I stopped before I said too much. "The anniversary of James's death is coming up in the next few months, probably why I'm thinking about him so much. What we had was good—really good—and I don't want to ever seem like I didn't love him completely and appreciate every single moment we had together. But I feel like a damn asshole when I think I wouldn't have all of this bringing me joy if he hadn't died."

"When did he die?" Justin asked as his hand caught mine and he laced our fingers together.

Rattling off the date in a trance as I remembered that horrific day, I barely noticed when Justin flinched. "You okay?"

"Yeah." He nodded and took a drink of his coffee. "You know I'll be there for you, however you need me that day. Just let me know."

I gave his hand a squeeze. "Thanks."

"So, James wouldn't have liked this place?" Justin asked.

I laughed. "Not even slightly. He may have been okay with the sauna and the amenities inside the cabin, but James was *not* a nature person. His idea of a weekend away would have been a museum, a Broadway show, and a wine tasting at the most upscale winery."

Justin's eyes went wide.

"That makes him sound like a stuck-up snob, but he wasn't at all. He was reserved and liked nice things, but he also loved to laugh and tease. He was just as happy reading a report for work in bed beside me as he would have been going to his favorite vintage car show." I said the words knowing I spoke one hundred percent truth. "But he didn't even blink an eye when I asked to do something he wasn't fond of." I shrugged. "As the years went by, we did less and less because work took over more and more, but James never stopped loving me and making me happy in our unconventional partnership."

"I mean, the museum, Broadway, and wine don't sound *bad*, just different. It's okay to have different interests and make concessions for your partner."

I nodded. "I just wish I'd forced us both to take more breaks. Maybe if I'd *made* him relax, he wouldn't have died."

Justin hummed softly. "I don't know. I didn't have the honor of knowing him, but from what you've said, forcing James to take a break would have been like attempting to force the sun not to shine.

A laugh caught in my throat and I swallowed thickly. "You have no idea."

"His death was *not* your fault." Justin leaned in to kiss my cheek. "I'm sorry you lost him. I wish I could have known him; I'm so grateful you had him and so many years together to love each other and be happy."

Tears stung my eyes. "I'm grateful for the years, too." I cocked my head and studied Justin. "He would have liked you."

"Yeah?" Justin's smile was pleased.

"Yeah. He would have loved your youthful enthusiasm and creativity."

Justin's hand came up to cup my cheek. "I know it's just a short time, but I hope I can make you even a fraction as happy as James made you. I'm grateful for the time we get to spend together. Never trying to take his place, please know that. But if James can't be here to make you smile and bring you happiness, I hope he's okay with me filling in for the time being. If that's okay with you."

Placing my empty mug on the railing of the deck, I wrapped Justin in my arms and poured every single bit of love I felt for the man into the kiss as I devoured his mouth and wished with every fiber of my being we could forget our end date.

"Thank you," I whispered against his lips when we broke apart. "I've done my best to move away from *What if I could bring him back* type thinking because it's useless. I *can't* and it's only a lesson in pain and heartache to make myself choose between the love and happiness I had with him and the new life I'm building here." *And the unexpected, all-consuming love I've discovered for you.* I wanted so badly to tell Justin how I felt, but I worried it would mess up the rest of our time together. I'd never thought I'd love again after James. Sure, I'd thought I'd maybe seek companionship, but never love. James had been my one true love, my soul mate, my forever.

So, why was my heart tugging and longing so hard for Justin?

Could a person have that type of love with more than one?

Can a person love pizza and beer with a friend just as much as they love wine and caviar with a different friend?

Food and drinks were completely different than matters of the heart.

Right?

I sighed when Justin tucked himself into me as I ran my hands up and down his back. I never wanted to betray James, never wanted to forget him or be untrue to his memory…but the thought of what I could have with Justin lit a fire in me and promised an adventure and happiness I hadn't even realized I longed for. Thinking about saying goodbye, letting Justin go at the end of our time together nearly brought me to my knees.

That had to mean something, right?

What would James say? What would he want me to do?

I kissed the top of Justin's head as James's face appeared in my mind. I smiled to think of his dry, cutting personality that served him so well in our business lives. Only *I* saw the other side of him, the dry, sarcastic, joking as he rolled his eyes when I wasn't thinking clearly, and the deep, unending love he had for me.

Morgan, my dear, dear man. Don't be an idiot. I've said it before and I'll say it again until you finally get it. I'm dead. You're not. Just as you'd never expect me to live the rest of my life alone and sad, I'd never expect it from you. He's young—so damn young, you scoundrel —but he makes you smile. He can never take away what we had and I love him for not trying to, but he's good for you and I want more than anything for you to be happy until we meet again. Don't miss your chance. Tell him how you feel.

Tucking away James's words for later, I jostled Justin in my arms. "Ready to get back to our baby?"

Once the cabin was locked and we piled into the Jeep, Justin reached for my hand. "Did you want to do something special for James?"

I took a deep breath. "I've been spreading a bit of his ashes with each passing year. I'll think about it. Nothing has seemed right so far when I think about it."

"Just let me know. Whether you need company or a day alone, I'm here."

I gave his hand a squeeze and did my best to categorize the mess of feelings sloshing around inside me.

The anniversary of James's death dawned bright and beautiful. Justin didn't complain once on our run and we breezed into Piping Hot ready to tackle whatever the day brought.

In the three months since our little getaway, Justin and I had grown closer in all aspects of our lives together. With the exception of a few nit-picky things here and there, we got along great at the shop and at home.

Piping Hot was running perfectly and we'd increased our profits in every one of the six months since we took over. Within the next half a year, Justin wanted a new espresso machine, a bean roaster, and smoothies. Being the good businessman he was, though, he was waiting and making sure each expense and next step was best for the shop.

There had yet to be any baked goods Justin made the customers didn't rave over and the Bundt cakes had been a huge success. Justin hoped to bring on another baker within the year to help with keeping up with demand and maybe making some items part of the standard menu rather than rotating.

At home, Justin and I were in perfect sync and I sometimes wondered if our end date was the reason for that. Didn't most couples think they'd be together forever and end up resenting each other, driving each other up the wall, and feeling smothered? Maybe since Justin and I knew we had only a short time together, we were able to appreciate the positives and ignore the negatives.

We spent most of our time together. Morning runs, shifts at the shop, dinners, and relaxing at home. Our sex life was amazing and I often felt as if I'd never get enough of Justin. But more than that, we seemed to truly just enjoy being around each other. We enjoyed cooking together, we liked a lot of the same shows and movies, we had fun going out and supporting local businesses, and we never failed to have a great time when visiting with Harley and Jo Ellen.

And yet, I'd still not told him how badly I didn't want it all to end.

He'd not mentioned anything either.

I was definitely going to tell him, I just hadn't picked the right time.

The anniversary of my late husband's passing didn't seem appropriate so I pushed the thoughts away and wondered how to honor James that day. I had a bit of his ashes in an urn and I thought of the wood line where Justin and I often saw wildlife. Would James want to be scattered there?

I huffed a laugh. Likely, no. He wasn't a fan of nature. But Briarton was my home and I wanted James to share in it.

Will you stay in Briarton once you and Justin go your own ways?

Justin and I hadn't talked about what would happen after we divorced—surprise, surprise. Despite our number one rule, we seemed pretty good at avoiding certain topics.

I had no plans to leave Briarton, but I did worry my heartache would be too heavy to allow me to stay.

But the thought of leaving what I'd built in the town was also heartbreaking.

Maybe I'd take the urn out later and see if somewhere in or around town felt like the right place to spread some of the ashes. If not, nothing said I *had* to do it. There was always next year or I could just keep the remaining ashes.

"Hey, taste this," Justin said, breaking into my thoughts as he pressed a fork to my mouth.

I took a bite and sighed as a burst of moist cake and sweet, creamy icing filled my mouth. "Oh my God, that's good. What is it?"

"I saw it on a cooking show. Instead of cupcakes, which we know our customers adore, it's a cake cup. Break up pieces of cake, layer the cake and globs of icing into a cup, add toppings if you want, and you have a cup of cake. A cake cup. Not something we'd have on the daily, but it could be fun to add to the rotation." Justin raised a brow as he waited on my reply.

"I love it." I leaned in and kissed him as the bells chimed over the front entrance.

"Welcome to Piping Hot," Sandy greeted the newcomer.

"Hi, I'm looking for Justin Wade," the customer said and I felt Justin tense beside me.

"You've got to be fucking kidding me," Justin growled.

"What's wrong?" I asked and peeked around the corner to see a very attractive young man with messy blond hair and an easy smile. "Who is that?"

"Sean." Justin ran a hand over his face.

Without a second's hesitation, I took his hand. "I can tell him to leave. I can go out there with you. I can tell him you're not here. Tell me what you need."

Justin took a deep breath and squeezed my hand. "Go with me?"

"Absolutely."

"There's my boy," Sean said with a huge smile as Justin and I emerged from the back.

"What do you want, Sean?" Void of emotion, Justin eyed his ex up and down.

"Okay, okay, I figured you'd be a little happier to see me, but I can see you're going to make me work for it." Sean threw a glance my way. "Who's your daddy?"

Wanting to throttle the man, I swallowed my angry growl and let Justin take the lead as I shot daggers at Sean.

"Sean, this is my husband, Morgan." Justin gave my hand a squeeze and I could almost hear him apologizing for using our marriage to needle Sean. "Morgan, someone I used to know."

"Ouch," Sean exclaimed, clutching a hand to his chest. "Harsh." He gave me the once over and leered. "Didn't know you had a thing for sexy silver foxes, Jus, but I approve."

"Why are you here?" Justin stood his ground.

"Crazy thing. Friend of a friend saw an article in some magazine about small-town Midwest living. Thought they recognized your name—didn't realize you'd left me high and dry, thought we were still together—and showed me the article wanting to know how my boyfriend was in this Podunk town while I'm hitting it big in the city."

Justin scoffed. "Yeah, *I* left *you* high and dry."

Sean shrugged. "Figured since it was your birthday, I'd come see what the hell you'd gotten yourself into and take you out for dinner."

Justin tensed beside me.

Wait, what? His birthday? *Today* was his birthday?

I couldn't exactly ask since his *husband* would know his birthday, but damn it. How did I not know that?

And then realization punched me in the gut. Justin knew the date of James's death was the same as his own birthday. Fuck. He didn't tell me because he was trying to be anything and everything I needed him to be as I mourned my dead husband—while not celebrating the birthday of my very much alive husband.

Fuck.

Temporary or not, Justin deserved to have his day celebrated and not overlooked because it happened to be the same day James died.

"We have a business to run," Justin told Sean coldly. "I'll have to pass. Thanks for stopping by."

Sean glanced my way. "I'm sure sugar daddy has something fancy planned, but let me at least buy you a cup of coffee so we can catch up."

Justin snorted. "I own a coffee shop. Try again."

"Lunch? Maybe not way out here in hick town, but let me buy you a meal." Sean turned on the charm and I could definitely see how the sleaze ball could weasel his way into pretty much anything.

"Buy me lunch?" Justin bristled. "With the money you stole from me? No, I'm sure you burned through that within a month, right? Where are you getting your cash these days? Got a few more unsuspecting souls on the hook to line your pockets?"

Sean held up his hands. "Look, babe. We talked about that. We both knew there'd be risks with the start-up; can't blame me that it went bust."

I folded my arms across my chest. "But he *can* blame you for taking his start-up money and ghosting him. Convenient you had no contracts or paper trail. Just a good man with a good idea who trusted a piece of shit to do the right thing and got screwed over in the process."

Sean, clearly used to getting what he wanted, gave me the side-eye and chose to ignore me as if I'd just go away. "Come on, Jus, let's go eat and catch up."

"Not interested. Please leave." Justin crossed his arms. "There's nothing in this town for you."

As if he couldn't believe his ears, Sean scowled as he studied Justin. "You're for real right now? You're going to pick Small Town, USA and a *coffee shop* over what we could have?"

Justin took a step toward Sean. "I'm going to take my

home, my dream, and my family over *anything* you and I ever had. Go."

Sean shook his head and walked out the door.

Justin ran a hand over his face. "Of all the fucking nerve."

I took his hand and led him to the office. "Are you okay?"

Justin nodded. "Yeah, just wasn't expecting to deal with that shit today. Or ever again, really."

"Why didn't you tell me it was your birthday?"

He blanched. "It felt wrong to talk about my birthday when it was the same day James died. I wanted the day to be whatever you needed it to be."

With my head spinning as I tried to think—about how to honor James, how to celebrate Justin—I could only shake my head. "Look, I need a bit. Can you handle the shop for the rest of the day?"

A quick look of something crossed Justin's face, but he gave a nod. "Yeah, not a problem. I'll see you at home later?"

Absently, I nodded. "Yeah, sounds good."

With plans bouncing around in my head, I gave a brief wave and headed out the door. Once home, I grabbed the small urn of James's ashes and headed out for a walk.

When I reached the little bench next to the open field and wood line, I sat and turned the urn around in my hands. "Don't really know what to do here," I said in a broken whisper. "You weren't supposed to die, weren't supposed to leave me here alone."

Only the breeze through the leaves, birds, and frogs answered.

"And I wasn't supposed to go and fall in love with someone else." I pressed my forehead to the urn. "Wasn't supposed to be this hard, this confusing."

What's so damn confusing about it? I'm dead. You fell for Justin. Do what you need to do with my damn ashes and go celebrate his birthday.

I chuckled at the words I knew James would say, almost as if I could hear his voice telling me to get my head out of my ass.

But was I just hearing the words I wanted to hear? Would James really have wanted me to move on and be happy without him?

I knew the answer to that before the question had even formed in my head.

Yes. James was the least selfish person I'd ever met. He *never* would have wanted me to be sad and alone after he passed.

Tapping the urn against my forehead, I muttered, "Think about it. You're letting what ifs and maybes and guilt take control over the reality of your situation. Fact: James is dead. Fact: He was your best friend and you loved him very much, but your heart is already proving it can love again. Fact: You could be happy with Justin—even if just for the remaining time on your deal."

Feeling like a crazy person for talking to a container of ashes, I pressed a kiss against the cool metal of the urn. "Thank you. I don't think I'm spreading your ashes anywhere today. I need more time to decide on the perfect place this year."

Imagining James wrapping me in a solid, warm hug, I took a deep breath. "I love you and will never, ever forget what we had. We grew up together, we discovered ourselves together, and we were exactly what each other needed at that time in our lives." Brushing a tear from the corner of my eye, I continued. "But it's a different time in my life now. There will always be a hole in my heart where you belong, but I love this place, I love the shop, and I love Justin. I may not know exactly how things are going to pan out with him, but I'm not going to spend my time mourning when I could be living." The words caught in my throat—as much as I meant them and knew they were what I needed, they still hurt. "Thank you for helping to make me into the man I am today and preparing me for the journey ahead of me."

After a few silent moments, I tucked the urn under my arm and headed back to my apartment. I placed the container on the bookshelf and texted Harley to see if I could come over for a bit.

I had a birthday party to plan.

It took quite a while to convince Jo and Harley that Justin did *not* want a big party.

"Morgan, dear, how in the world are you just planning a party on the day of his actual birthday?" Jo Ellen clasped her hands. "Harley and I were going to take him out for dinner in a few days. We assumed you had big plans."

"Sharing birthdays just wasn't something we'd done yet. Probably too caught up in getting married and taking over the shop." I prayed they wouldn't dig any deeper because I truly had no good excuses as to how and why I didn't know my husband's birthday. "We just weren't thinking about details like that."

Jo and Harley both eyed me for a long moment as if they most definitely didn't believe me.

I shrank under their gazes. "Look, today is also the day James died. I feel terrible enough I didn't know it was Justin's birthday. Sean popped into the shop and shook Justin up. I just want to plan something and spend his day with him. Can you help?"

That information broke them from their trance and they immediately stepped into action.

"Okay, let's do flowers, dinner, wine, and dessert. What's

a gift you'd like to get for him? Something he's been wanting?" Jo clapped her hands together as she took charge.

"There's an espresso machine he's been eyeing for the shop. If you two can help set up the food and wine, I'll order the machine and get the flowers."

Jo waved me off. "You take care of the machine. We'll do the rest. Go home, get the gift ordered. Clearly, you won't have it for today, so make a nice card and put a picture of the machine in it. Clean the house. Set up a special area for watching a movie or something. Get some candles to make it all romantic." She shook her head. "I would have preferred a big celebration, but…"

"We know Justin isn't the type to want the spotlight on him," Harley interrupted. "Let's get a move on. We don't have a lot of time. Any preference on the meal or dessert?"

Grateful for their help, I shook my head. "No, maybe just something we wouldn't fix a lot here. If possible, dessert should be something Justin doesn't make often."

We said goodbye and I knew I'd done the right thing by enlisting their help, even if it meant I had to admit I didn't know it was my husband's birthday. As I walked down the steps of Harley's house, Jo called out to me.

"Morgan?"

I turned around and saw them standing, arm in arm. "Yeah?"

"We both know what it's like to lose someone you love and the struggle with moving on. It's okay to be sad and miss James. It's also okay to love Justin and make a happy life with him," Jo Ellen said.

With a nod, afraid I wouldn't be able to speak around the lump in my throat, I gave a quick wave. It helped so much that others understood what I was feeling. It didn't take away the difficulties, but it made me feel not so alone.

Rushing home, I stood in the living room for a moment as

I decided what to do first. As if James was watching with a knowing smile, I glanced toward the urn before turning my eyes toward the sky. "You're enjoying this, aren't you?"

With the memory of his chuckle filling my head and a warmth spreading through my heart, I set to work ordering the new espresso machine, cleaning the house, setting up a little movie-watching-nest on the couch, and searching through a stockpile of candles to find scents that would blend well.

About an hour before Justin was scheduled to be home, Jo and Harley showed up with dinner, dessert, wine, and three of the most gorgeous bouquets of flowers I'd ever seen.

"Wow, thank you both so much." I took the items from them, not wanting to rush them off, but hoping they didn't linger because I still had a lot to do.

"We won't stay long," Harley assured. "Just wanted to check if you needed any help with anything."

"No, I'm good. I'm going to shower, get dinner in the oven, and do final touches." I hugged Jo Ellen and Harley. "Thank you so much for your help. We're so blessed to call you family."

Once they were gone, I checked the instructions on the food. I had just enough time for a shower before I needed to slip everything into the oven to warm. Filet mignon with a béarnaise sauce, garlic butter mushrooms, cheesy baked asparagus, lemony herb couscous awaited us for dinner and a vanilla bean crème brûlée for dessert. I wasn't sure, but I thought Justin had the right tool for caramelizing the sugar on top. Jo had included a rich chardonnay with the meal.

After my shower, I checked the time and wrapped up all the last-minute tasks before settling in to wait for Justin. As the apartment filled with the scents from the candles, the meal, and the flowers, a feeling of anxious apprehension washed over me.

Was it too much?

Not enough?

Would Justin think I was trying too hard?

Should I have focused more on James?

I cast a look toward the bookshelf where the urn sat just as the door opened.

No, James was the past—a forever cherished and loved part of my past, but still, my past—and Justin was the present. If I had anything to do with it, Justin would also be my future.

I stood to meet him and immediately knew something was wrong.

"Hey, happy birthday was the plan, but *what's wrong* seems more appropriate," I reached for his hand just as a choked sob escaped him. "Hey, hey, what's wrong?"

"You left," Justin whispered.

"Just to clear my head and get ready for your birthday." My stomach plummeted at the thought of upsetting Justin.

He chuckled humorlessly. "I see that. *Now.* But all day long, all I could think about was how badly Sean threw me for a loop, how it was the day James died, and the fact you left. I feel ridiculous, but it reminded me of when Sean took off." Justin tucked himself into my chest. "I respect that this day is for James. I'd never expect you to pick me over him. It just freaked me out when you walked away. And I know that's stupid when this isn't even real, but it all just added up to too much. I worried I'd get here and you'd be gone."

I kissed the top of his head and ignored the mixture of hope and dread in my chest—was it possible Justin sounded upset when he mentioned our temporary marriage? "I'm so damn sorry. I didn't even stop to think how it would look to you. I took James's ashes for a walk and talked to him. Then I admitted to Jo and Harley I somehow didn't know my own husband's birthday and asked them to help me set up an impromptu party for you."

Justin jerked back, his eyes wide. "We're having a party?"

"No," I said with a chuckle and kissed his nose. "We're having dinner, dessert, and wine. The only guests are us, flowers, candles, a gift, and a movie on our couch—alone. Promise."

"Sounds like the best birthday ever." Justin relaxed against me. "What did you and James talk about?"

My heart clenched at how sincere Justin sounded. He truly wasn't the type to expect me to forget about James completely. Maybe it was because of the way our relationship had come together in such an unconventional way, but Justin never seemed jealous of my life before him.

I had him sit while I put dinner together and told him about the conversation. "It was a good talk. Trying to explain to Jo and Harley how I didn't know it was your birthday was a lot less enjoyable."

Justin winced. "Yeah, that was a major miss in our planning. Sorry about that. And I'm sorry for not telling you my birthday is today." He took a long sip of the wine. "Ohhh, that's good." Tapping his fingers on the table as I plated our food, Justin went on. "How crazy is it that my birthday is the same day James died?"

"Yeah, definitely weird. Honestly, I think it would have been even weirder if you'd both shared a birthday. Or if you'd been born the same day he died." I shrugged. "As it is, it's strange, but kinda in an interesting way."

Justin thought about that for a while. "Yeah, I can see that." He took a deep breath. "What's for dinner? It smells amazing."

We dug into our meal—which was absolutely delicious—and Justin had a lot of fun adding sugar to our crème brûlée and caramelizing it.

"The candles are great and I love the flowers. I'm going to take one bouquet to work and leave the other two here." Justin savored bites of dessert as he snipped and arranged the flowers into vases. Then he turned to me with shy smile. "I heard there was a gift?"

I laughed and handed him the card. "You'll have to deal with this for now, but it ships soon."

Justin opened the card and gasped. "Are you fucking kidding me? You got me the espresso machine? No way, this is *way* too much."

"Too late, it's already ordered. More hassle to cancel than to just let me buy you something nice."

"Thank you," Justin said as he grabbed my chin and kissed me soundly. "I better plan on getting you that sauna for your birthday if I wanna match this."

"We'll see. You wanna watch a movie?"

Justin bit his lip. "Is there an option for movie later and bedroom now?"

"We can make that work. Anything in particular you're wanting?" I all but dragged him to the bedroom. While I would have been satisfied with a movie, Justin's idea sounded much better.

"Maybe we see if we can make the fantasy come true?" Justin wagged his brow and I laughed. "Or at least have lots of fun trying."

In the time since we'd allowed a sexual component into our marriage of convenience, we'd tried more than once to make Justin's dirty fantasy come true. The problem was—if you could even count it as a problem—I'd never been able to hold off on orgasming long enough for Justin to blow his load in me and then let me fuck him. "It's worth a try, I definitely won't complain." There were no losers in the scenario.

"Get naked," Justin ordered.

As much as I loved topping Justin, I also adored every

single second of him being inside me. There was *nothing* like feeling him come in me, but I also couldn't get enough of sliding deep into his ass and unloading as he clenched around me. It had taken me until age forty-eight, but I'd definitely discovered the joys of being vers.

We stripped down and Justin tossed the lube on the mattress before pushing me to my back and crawling on top. "Happy birthday to me," he murmured against my lips before kissing me and rocking our cocks together.

Justin pressed hot, wet kisses down my body and had me begging him to suck my cock, but he just turned me over and spread my ass. It had taken a while to get to a point where I didn't need loads of prepping and stretching, but Justin had been patient and seemed to truly love getting my ass ready to take him. As his tongue worked me open, he pressed a finger against me until I whimpered.

"Patience," Justin teased, licking around my hole. After lubing a finger, he slipped in first one and then two, stretching my muscle all while avoiding my balls, my cock, and my prostate.

"This is torture," I complained.

"Yeah, but it's *good* torture," Justin said.

"Says you. You're not the one dying for someone to suck your cock." I shifted, trying my best to get Justin's fingers deeper to stroke that bundle of nerves.

"You know it's for the best. The plan is always to get *me* to come first then you can fuck me. The less stimulated you are, the better our chances."

"Two fingers in my ass doesn't exactly scream less stimulated," I said on a groan.

"Touché," Justin said as he slid from my ass and positioned himself so his cock was right at my face. "Suck me. I'm gonna jack myself and right before I come, I'll fuck into you."

I greedily opened my mouth and took his shaft deep, loving the way he pressed against my throat. When he was close, Justin pulled from my mouth and moved behind me, lifting my ass, and spreading me open before he gripped his cock and stroked.

"Fuck, I'm close. You ready? I'm gonna slide into you and blow my load." Justin panted as he fucked his fist.

"Fuck, yeah," I groaned. Being on my knees made it a lot less likely I'd come, even if I preferred the face-to-face position of being on my back.

As Justin's grunts and groans increased, I pressed my ass back and hissed when his blunt head touched my hole. With one long thrust, Justin slid into me, taking my breath away with the stinging stretch of his invasion.

My cock deflated just enough for me to think maybe this time we had a chance as Justin gripped my hips and thrust hard and fast five times. As his cock pulsed his release and Justin groaned, I savored the throbbing heat of his cock filling my ass.

"Oh fuck," Justin breathed out as he collapsed on top of me. "You okay?"

"I'm good," I answered. "You?"

"Be better once you're fucking me with my jizz dripping from your ass."

Groaning, I shifted under him. "You gonna be able to take it after you already came?"

Justin nodded and moved to his back, spreading his legs in glorious invitation. "Fuck me. And I wanna know when my cum drips out of your hole."

What was it about this random dirty fantasy that always got both of us so worked up? Whatever it was, we'd had a hell of a good time working up to it.

I smeared pre-cum around the head of my dick as I lubed Justin's hole and slicked my dick. "Tell me if it's too much." I wasn't sure I could take a cock in my ass after an orgasm, so I didn't want to put him in an uncomfortable position.

"Get in me," Justin demanded as he opened his legs wider.

Pressing the head of my cock against his hole, I worked my way in inch-by-inch as I savored the tight hold he had on me. When my balls were flush against his skin, I waited a moment for Justin's body to adjust.

"I'm good. Move." Justin wrapped his legs around my waist and urged me to lean in so we were chest-to-chest. "Fuck me."

My thrusts began slow and steady, but the tight heat of Justin's body spurred me to move harder and quicker. When a warm dampness trickled from my hole and down my leg, I tensed. "Fuck, I can feel it. You're dripping from my ass."

Justin groaned and tightened his legs as he took his reawakening cock in hand. "Oh fuck, yeah. That's gonna make me come again. Love thinking about my cum in your ass." He whimpered as I thrust hard and deep. "Fuck, yeah. Come in me, wanna feel your cock unload."

Wrapping my arms around him and anchoring myself under his shoulders, I increased my speed even as I savored the wet, sticky mess dripping from my hole. Knowing I'd hit the right spot when Justin bucked his hips and grunted, I thrust over and over until my body tensed and my cock throbbed its release. More cum leaked from my hole as I unloaded in Justin's ass.

Justin clenched around me and spilled droplets between us with a soft whimper.

Sliding my spent cock from his body, I bent to lick cum from his belly before capturing his mouth and coating his tongue with his release.

When we finally caught our breaths, Justin chuckled. "Holy shit. Happy birthday to me is right. And I can't even tell anyone about the very best birthday gift I've ever received."

I snorted. "Well, I mean, you *could*, but it might get kinda awkward." I kissed him again, loving the warm pliant touch of his body against mine. "I love that sex with me beats out an espresso machine.

"The espresso machine *is* amazing. But *that*? That was mind-blowing, life-altering, fantasy-fulfilling sex." Justin nuzzled his nose against mine. "But if anyone asks, I'll just tell them about the espresso machine. It's safer that way."

"Pretty sure Briarton has no interest in our own little porn scene."

Justin laughed. "I don't know. I have a feeling there are some kinky fuckers around here. Just don't *ever* let me find out Jo and Harley are getting kinky. I can *not* handle that visual."

"Didn't Harley say Jo is pretty quirky in the bedroom? I bet she's got kinks galore," I teased. "Wonder if she likes to have sex with her Birkenstocks on. Nothing else, just the Jesus sandals."

"Oh my God, stop." Justin's eyes were wide.

"Maybe she uses her bracelets on Harley. Blows him with her bracelets around his dick."

Justin slapped his hands to his ears. "Stop it. That's so wrong. I can *not* think of them in a sexual way. Just eeww, no."

Laughing, I hugged him close and kissed him soundly. "We are a gross, sticky mess. Let's shower and then we can watch a movie. Even birthday boys have work tomorrow."

"Thank you so much for such a special birthday."

"I'm sorry I freaked you out by leaving. I was so focused on doing the right thing by James *and* giving you a special day, I didn't even think about how it might have come across for you." I gripped his chin. "Sean is an absolute douche and

I'd *never* treat you the way he did. I'm sorry he threw you for such a loop today. But I gotta say, I loved the way you shut him down. You are so much better and stronger than him."

"Thank you. Back when he took my money and left, I wasn't. But I definitely feel like I've learned a lot about myself since coming to Briarton. I no longer feel like I'm not good enough or I'm only worth guys like Sean." Justin kissed me, long and slow, and I allowed myself to think maybe, just *maybe*, I was part of the positive changes in Justin's life.

FIFTEEN

JUSTIN

AS OUR ONE-YEAR end date loomed closer—seriously, how had over nine months passed in the blink of an eye? —I tried to figure out a way to tell Morgan I didn't want our marriage to end. I was willing to do whatever it took to keep us together, but my biggest fear was Morgan didn't feel the same.

We *needed* to talk about how we were going to handle the shop, but we'd perfected the art of avoidance when it came to certain topics.

With less than three months left in our little deal, I knew I *had* to man-up and tell him how I felt. But I buried myself in the shop—baking, menus, coffee and tea rotations—and how perfect our life was together.

So what if it was fake? So what if it was ending soon?

If I ignored the truth maybe we could just forget all about the end date and keep on with our little set-up indefinitely.

I snorted as I slid a pan of cinnamon rolls from the oven. I knew damn well life didn't work that way. I knew I had to talk to him, even if it turned out he didn't feel the same. But

I selfishly wanted to keep our happy little bubble for as long as possible.

Honestly, sometimes I thought *maybe* Morgan felt the same as me. He was the most attentive, caring, generous man I'd ever known, and I adored every moment of my time with him. Surely, he couldn't treat me so well if he didn't feel the same, right?

Each passing day with Morgan had brought us closer and made me certain we could give it a real go. Even when we were dealing with baking mishaps, shifts needing covered, spilled milk, explosions of coffee grounds all over the floor, and the occasional cranky customer, Morgan and I played off each other and never missed a beat.

And it wasn't just in the shop. At home, we meshed and had practically perfected our down time. I'd finally admitted to him I *maybe* looked forward to our morning runs, but I shut him down quickly when he mentioned training for a half-marathon.

We talked about our day, our friends and family, shows, movies, books, hobbies. We'd started a garden out back and we'd been looking for trees that would be best for planting in the yard. When either of us had an off day, we talked about it and either cheered the other one up or gave each other space.

I truly could not have asked for a better husband and partner.

Except we'd agreed from the beginning it wasn't real.

Soon, we'd sign the real contract of sale. Piping Hot would be ours.

And we'd go our separate ways.

Right?

What would that even look like?

It was hard to fathom. How would I just move out of what had so easily become *our* house? How would I not smack his ass and press a kiss to his lips when I passed him in the office? How would I sleep without him by my side?

Not to mention the fallout that would come from us divorcing after buying Piping Hot from Jo Ellen free and clear. I had a feeling that would get highly awkward and I hated putting our little crew through that.

I slammed a drawer harder than was necessary. There was no more pussy-footing around it. I had to tell Morgan I didn't want our marriage to end. If he didn't feel the same, I'd be heartbroken, but I couldn't just keep lying to myself and him. Couldn't keep playing the what if and worst-case scenario games.

"What did that drawer do to you?" Morgan asked, trying to joke around, as he entered the kitchen.

Waving him off because I immediately saw something else on his face, I asked, "What's wrong? Why do you look like you've come to tell me coffee has become illegal?"

Morgan snorted, but he took my hands in his.

"Harley called me. He wanted me to tell you your mother and oldest sister are at his house."

My stomach dropped. Like seriously hit the floor and just sat on my feet in a quivering blob. "What? Why?" I hated the way my voice squeaked.

"I'm not completely sure. Harley said to tell you and let you decide if you wanted to go see them. I'm here if you want to go, but I support you completely if you don't want to." Morgan gave my hand a squeeze.

I thought about the information. "It's really weird my *mother* is here. Usually Dad comes to see Harley. Not often, but he's been here a few times over the years that I can remember. I honestly don't know if Mom has *ever* come to Briarton. I know Laura has been here—all the kids used to come, but my siblings hated it here. I was the only one who looked forward to every single summer and holiday I got to spend here with Harley." I babbled as the shock sank in and curiosity grew.

"It's up to you whether or not we go. Harley can tell you what they came for if you don't want to see them."

I shook my head. "Mom has never liked Harley and the feeling is pretty mutual. I hate to think of Harley having to deal with her himself."

Morgan chuckled. "Well, I'm pretty sure I heard Jo Ellen in the background so he's not alone. You know she can stand her ground enough for the both of them, but I doubt Harley would have much trouble either." He scowled. "I know your family hasn't been the best to you. Seems like they kinda wrote you off when you didn't conform to their ideals of how to live your life. That was *their* loss, you don't owe them anything."

"Deep down, I know that," I said. Dropping Morgan's hands, I shivered and rubbed my arms. "I don't know why, but I've got a bad feeling about this. My parents or siblings coming to visit is never a fun time, but the fact Mom is here makes me think something is wrong. I think we should go over there and see what's up." I paused with a scowl. "But I know family drama isn't something we agreed to, I don't expect you to deal with any of my family shit."

"Don't even think about it. I'm going." Morgan pulled me close and kissed me. "Let's finish up here real quick and let the crew know we won't be back today."

An hour later, I was grateful for Morgan's presence by my side.

As my mother vacillated between sneering at our joined hands, making angry demands, and wiping away tears I wasn't even sure were real, I clung to Morgan. Thanking my lucky stars for Jo Ellen and Harley, I asked my mother to tell me once again why she'd come to Briarton. My sister, Laura, appeared both bored and inconvenienced to have made the trip.

Mom sniffed and eyed Morgan before glancing toward Jo Ellen. "I'd prefer to keep this a family conversation."

Harley cracked his neck and took an audible breath. "Jo is more family than some will ever be. She stays."

"Morgan is my husband. He stays." I lifted my chin in challenge while gripping Morgan's hand tightly. The return squeeze was just the encouragement I needed. Never mind the fact I was using our relationship in ways it had never been intended.

Laura scoffed. "How did that even happen?" She eyed our joined hands. "Is he rich? You got screwed over by that last douche and decided a sugar daddy was your best bet? Seriously, Justin, he's basically our father's age."

I gaped at my oldest sister. Laura and I were likely the least close of all my siblings. She had no children and had basically been leader of my parents' entourage since she was a preteen. She was the quintessential snobby rich girl and my parents had doted on her, given her everything—as long as it upped their reputation and got them in the spotlight—and groomed her to be a trophy wife. So far, from what I'd heard last time I'd seen my dad, Laura hadn't been willing or able to land a husband.

Looking at her now, a judgmental sneer and confused glaze in her eyes, I figured she'd eventually find someone willing to put up with her. She wasn't very bright, she went through money like it was water, and she contributed pretty much nothing to society. But I knew there were men out there who would look past all of that and marry her to have the arm candy. It would be a farce of a marriage—Laura scheming up ways to get his money, likely while he had several mistresses—but, really, who was I to judge a messed-up marriage?

Glancing at Morgan, I chastised myself. No, what we had may have been sudden and unconventional, but it would never be only about money or filled with cheating.

"My marriage is none of your business." I turned toward my mom. "Tell me again why you're here."

"Your father is very ill and, as the oldest son, it's your responsibility to be there for your family," Mom explained again.

I'd hoped I'd just misunderstood her the first time, but no, I'd heard it correctly.

Fighting off the clenching of my chest—truly, I had no ill-will toward my family and would never wish for them to be sick or unhappy. I just had no interest in being involved in their big-city, jet-setting, snooty, rich people ways.

But my dad was sick? Not something I wanted to hear.

"Mom, I want to hear more about Dad, but you're speaking as if this is some sort of royal family situation. As the eldest son? The son the rest of you gladly wrote off as a worthless, small-town bumpkin who would never amount to anything because I was happy with a simpler life…"

A tiny gasp escaped my mother. "We simply wanted what was best for you, dear. You could have had all the money you ever needed, traveled the world, never worked a day in your life. Instead, you snubbed your nose at what your *family* could offer—what a slap in the face to have our own son turn his back on our generosity. We were so embarrassed—how does one explain to the upper level of society a member of our own family has chosen a simple life over what we have to offer?"

I scoffed. "Mom, do you even hear yourself?" Shaking my head, I realized the argument was pointless. Laura's empty head had most certainly come from my mother and talking sense to a woman who thought a *simple life* meant degrading yourself to living in the middle-class would get me nowhere.

"Never mind. I have a happy, fulfilling, *good* life here in Briarton. I'm a grown man and I made my choice to live like a normal person many years ago. For the longest time, I worried myself sick trying to be what you and Dad wanted me to be while still being happy. But that's just not me." I leaned forward, elbows on my knees, grateful Morgan's hand quickly came to rest on my lower back. "I have no responsibilities to you—eldest son or not. Now, tell me about Dad."

"Your father couldn't even make this trip himself due to his medical condition. He's bedridden and I fear depression is eating away at him." Mom dabbed a tissue at the corner of her eye.

Shit.

I didn't want to hear my dad was sick.

"What's wrong with him?" A million thoughts ran through my head. Cancer? Diabetes? Heart disease? Autoimmune disease?

"He's developed gout—it's a very painful disease and makes it nearly impossible for him to walk. He's had to cancel social appearances, overseas travel, and many a dinner due to his condition."

The pressure in my chest eased slightly. I'd actually read about gout a few months ago when one of our customers got the diagnosis from their doctor. I knew it to be a form of arthritis and it caused very painful joints, especially in the big toe. If left untreated, gout could get worse and *could* develop into something life threatening, but most people with the condition—with proper treatment and a few lifestyle changes—lived long, fairly normal lives.

I didn't like to think of my father in pain, but knowing his medical condition wasn't a death-sentence eased my mind a bit. "I hate to hear that. What treatments are the doctors suggesting?"

"Well," Mom sniffed, "they've started him on a couple medications that do seem to provide relief, but he continues to have flare-ups and he's miserable."

"Is Dad following what the doctors suggest as far as changes he can make to help ease the condition?" I knew from what our customer, Ed, had said that exercise, cutting back on alcohol, and adjusting his diet were suggestions his doctors had made.

"It's all stuff and nonsense. Asking a man like your father to exercise more? He was playing daily rounds of golf and now he can't walk from the clubhouse to the first green." Mom wrung her hands. "A man should be allowed to have a satisfying meal and enjoy a beer with his friends, don't you think?"

Wow, I hadn't realized my mother was such an enabler.

"Mom, from the little I know of gout, exercise and losing weight could definitely help." My dad was *busy*, but I wouldn't call him active if that made any sense. "Walking the golf course is great, but some aerobic exercise could help."

"He can barely walk!" Mom exclaimed.

Laura rolled her eyes and I raised my brow.

She shrugged. "He's been sick for like a year and I know he's in pain. But the medications help a lot and he's had like three flares in that time. So yes, when he's in a flare, he is mostly in bed, but it's not like he's been bedridden for a year at a time."

I cocked my head at Mom. "So, he's still having flare-ups and my understanding is those are terribly painful. But outside of the flare-ups—and the fact he won't make changes to possibly reduce those—he's doing well with the treatment?"

Mom shot an annoyed look toward her oldest daughter. "Your father is a man accustomed to the finer things in life."

Harley snorted and covered it with a cough.

With a lift of her chin, Mom continued, "He should not be made to give up what he loves. For God sake, one doctor even suggested he purchase a cane for when walking is difficult. A cane? Can you even imagine?" She shivered.

Wow, both of my parents were going to be in for big shocks as they got older.

I took a breath. "I'm very sorry to hear Dad is suffering. I know it's a painful disease. I *do* wish he'd make some of the changes being suggested. Exercise in addition to golfing—when he's not in a flare, he could definitely get some workouts in. Cutting back on alcohol wouldn't be a bad idea overall—limit the number of beers with buddies, do some research on which alcohol is the least harmful for his condition and stick to that when drinking after dinner." I shrugged. "My friend Ed has gout and he's working to cut out certain foods. He's already noticing a difference."

"Your friend *Ed* lives a very different lifestyle," Mom bit out.

I took yet another long, calming breath. "True, but the treatment for this condition doesn't change based on where a person lives or how much money they have."

The look on Mom's face showed she didn't like what I was saying.

"I'm glad the medications are helping. I'm sure your friends will understand when Dad can't attend certain functions if he's feeling bad. Hopefully, you can convince him to do a few of the things the doctors are suggesting and he can get even more relief." I pursed my lips. "I'm still not sure what it is you want from me."

"You need to come home. We'll pay for the move and get you out of whatever ridiculous notion you have about owning a business. When your father is unable to travel, you'll go in his place."

I gaped. Seriously, I felt a lot like a fish out of water in this conversation. "First, why would you even want me there? Second, what about Eric?" My brother was a lot more like my father than me, but possibly a bit less pretentious thanks to the girl he married.

Mom waved her hand. "Eric has a family and a job."

"I have a family and a job," I deadpanned.

She scoffed. "You know what I mean. You should be with us, take your proper place in society."

I shook my head as Morgan ran a calming hand up and down my back. "No, I really *don't* know what you mean, but that's neither here nor there. I don't understand the *why* behind you wanting me to join you—I'm not the face you want representing the family to your high-society friends. I'm not at all interested in living in the city or traveling all over the world just to attend swanky parties and spend money. I have a life here. A life I love. I'm a business owner." I ran a hand through my hair. "I'm sorry Dad is sick, but I won't be joining you. My life is here."

Mom stared at me in disbelief. I got the feeling she wasn't used to being told no. "You owe us this."

"Excuse me?" Morgan interrupted.

Mom shot him a look of disdain.

"Please explain to me how your son—the one you've never accepted, the son you've ridiculed and looked down on because he wasn't like you—owes you a damn thing," Morgan demanded.

"This is a family affair and none of your business," Mom bit out.

"You're right, Sally," my grandpa said, cutting off my angry retort at the way Mom spoke to Morgan.

Mom looked smug.

"This *is* a family affair. You chose your family a long time ago and you made it clear it didn't include Justin unless he changed who he was to fit into the mold you envisioned."

Harley crossed his arms over his chest. "Justin and I chose our own little family and we're happy to have Morgan and Jo Ellen as part of it. While I hate to hear my son is suffering from a medical issue, I don't like that you've come here using his pain as a guise to get Justin to come home. I'm not sure what your endgame is—hell, I'm not even sure if *you* know what your endgame is other than just getting your way—but I'd like to ask you to leave."

Mom gasped. "Excuse me? You can't force me away from my son."

Harley nodded. "You're right. I can't. But I can ask you to leave my house. If Justin would like to continue this conversation with you, he's welcome to. As for me, I'm done with it."

Mom stood and snapped her fingers at Laura who pulled her head from her phone and stood with a huff. How was my oldest sister such a child? It truly bothered me to see what she was like thanks to the way Mom and Dad raised her—what would her life be like when they finally married her off to some billionaire with more money than sense?

"Come on, Justin, let's go," my mother said.

I stood and her face lit with triumph. "No, Mom. This is my home. I'll give Dad a call—I'm truly sorry he's been sick. But I'm not leaving with you. I'm not joining you as the face of the family. Whatever that even means—I'm pretty sure your reputation isn't in need of a gay baker and coffee shop owner."

It felt as if I *should* say it was nice to see her or thanks for coming by, but none of those were true, so I kept my mouth shut as Mom huffed and yanked on Laura's arm. "Let's go. If we leave now we can make the flight to Milan."

And with that, my mom and sister were gone.

Harley, Jo Ellen, Morgan, and I stood in stunned silence for a bit.

"What the hell was that?" I murmured.

Grandpa slapped me on the back. "I'm not sure, but you did good. You know I'd never begrudge you the chance to spend time with your family and I'd never judge you for it. But you don't owe them anything and if you choose to visit them, travel with them, join them in any way, it should be because *you* want it, not because they're bullying you into it."

I shook my head. "It took a while, but I've realized I'm happier without them in my life. All those years trying to be what they wanted me to be were miserable and exhausting. I hate Dad is sick, but I can't for the life of me figure out why they'd want me with them for anything."

Jo tutted. "I doubt Sally even knows that. She's a woman used to getting what she wants *and* coming up with projects when she's bored or needs to land herself in the spotlight again. I wouldn't be surprised if she's feeling neglected when your father is unable to travel and she decided she could get some attention by *saving* her poor, lost son."

Morgan put an arm around me. "That sounds as plausible as any other reason I can think of." After pressing a kiss against my head, he turned to Jo and Harley. "I think we've had enough excitement for today. I'm going to get this one home."

A couple hours later, I nearly fell off the couch when Morgan told me to come eat dinner. I *may* have opened a bottle of wine when we got home and I *may* have done a bit more gulping than sipping as I rambled on and on about my family.

"Whoa, easy there," Morgan said with a chuckle as he helped me to my feet. "Let's get some food in you to soak up that wine."

As much as I knew I'd regret it in the morning, I was too far gone to even care and I poured myself another glass before offering the wine to Morgan.

"I'll pass. One overindulger is enough for the evening," Morgan said with a kiss to my cheek as I sat to eat a meal designed to hopefully sober me up.

Of course, eating while already drunk and adding more wine on top was not the best plan.

When we made our way to bed—okay, when Morgan basically carried me to bed—fairly early, but the day and alcohol had taken their toll, I stripped clumsily and climbed onto the mattress.

"Come fuck me," I said, spreading my legs and stroking my cock. "Doubt I can get hard enough to fuck you."

Morgan frowned. "Probably best if we're both sober for that." He shucked his clothes and climbed onto the bed next to me.

I gripped his chin. "I'm drunk, but not incoherent. Want me to explain to you the differences in coffee beans? I can do it and make perfect sense. I'm not so far gone I can't give consent. In fact, I could likely give you this month's profit report without even opening my laptop." Brushing a kiss over his lips and smiling when he groaned and rocked his already-hard cock against me, I went on. "Yes, I've had too much to drink. Yes, I'm drunk and shouldn't be doing any driving or operating heavy machinery. But I'm coherent enough to give consent and tell you I want your cock buried in my ass."

Morgan hesitated.

"Look," I continued, "the hangover tomorrow is going to suck hairy donkey balls. At least give me something that makes it worth it. Because right now, the only thing to go along with getting this drunk is my mother and that's not going to be comforting in the morning." I kissed him, teasing his lips and tongue, exploring his mouth and savoring his flavor.

"Give me the recipe for your favorite cookies," Morgan said, gasping as he broke away from the kiss.

I launched into a reciting of every single ingredient and measurement for my to-die-for butter cookies with buttercream icing as Morgan stared at me in disbelief.

"See," I said with a triumphant smile. "I'm definitely drunk, but I know exactly what's going on."

I felt the moment Morgan gave in to my begging and bit my lip as he reached into the drawer for lube.

Stretched out on my side with Morgan at my back, I bent my left leg and shifted slightly to offer him my ass. When the slick, blunt head of his cock pressed against my hole, I shivered and moaned, savoring the stretch and fullness. Morgan pumped into me, slow and sure, as he tipped my chin and made love to my mouth as he claimed my body.

Despite my inebriated state, orgasm found me thanks to Morgan's stroking fist and agonizingly slow thrusting. When he recovered from his throbbing release, Morgan slid from my body and wrapped me in his arms.

As my swampy brain fought off sleep, I cuddled into him. "I think I love you and I don't want this thing to come to an end."

Morgan froze and I heard his swallow. "Um, that's probably something we should talk about when we're both sober. For sure."

I nodded, deliriously happy and sleepy. "Yeah. Probably. Just wanted you to know."

A few moments later, I thought Morgan whispered something, but I was already drifting off to sleep.

SIXTEEN

MORGAN

"IF YOU EVEN HINT AT making me run this morning, I will murder you," Justin grumbled as he staggered to the kitchen the next morning.

Chuckling, I handed him a cup of coffee. "You survived the shower. Feeling any better?"

Justin had slept like the dead and hadn't even stirred when my alarm went off. I, on the other hand, had barely slept a wink and spent my lonely run contemplating Justin's drunk words.

Before he'd claimed to love me and not want our situation to come to an end, I'd been working out a plan. One I was hoping would seem romantic and end with Justin and I staying together.

But then he'd said what he'd said and I wasn't sure how to handle it.

Approach him about it?

Ignore it?

If I approached him, he could deny it.

If I ignored what he'd said, he would maybe think I didn't care.

It was likely best to give him an opening and see if he wanted to discuss anything. No matter what his response, I was going through with my plans the night before we were scheduled to sign the final contract of sale. Things would have just been easier if he hadn't been drunk when he'd declared his love for me.

On the other hand, his words—inebriated state or not—gave me hope.

"Huh?" Justin grunted.

"I said you survived the shower. Are you feeling any better?"

"Nearly drowned myself. Got sick and sat down. Then I laid down. It wasn't pretty." He shuddered and sipped at his coffee. "Also, my head is going to explode. Let's get to the shop; I'll eat there. Hopefully, the pain medication will have kicked in a bit by then."

"You need to double your water intake today, maybe throw in a sports drink, too." I wrapped my arms around his waist, pressing my front against his back as he stared out the kitchen window. Burying my nose in his freshly washed hair, I breathed in deep. "Missed you on my run."

Justin groaned. "Sorry. I barely survived the shower, a run would have done me in." After setting his cup on the counter, he turned in my arms. "Who in the hell drinks that much wine? I've been a lot drunker in my day, but I'm not sure I've ever felt *this* hungover. My whole body aches."

"Wanna stay home?"

He shook his head. "No, there's inventory to do, orders to place, and baking to do."

"You just wanna use your espresso machine," I teased.

Justin's eyes lit up. "Have you *seen* it? It's gorgeous and works like it's been spelled with magic."

"Ohhh, magic-infused coffee drinks. Maybe that can be our new thing."

He laughed as he tucked his head into the crook of my neck. "Not gonna stay home, but I very well may cut out early. Damn, is this what hangovers are like as you get older?"

"Yeah, just wait until you're my age, they're basically death." I chuckled as he groaned. "You think we should talk about things that were said last night?"

There was no mistaking the way Justin's body tensed. After a moment, he shook his head. "Nah, I was drunk. Who knows what I said. Best to just figure it was all nonsense."

Well, that was a punch to the gut, but I wasn't going to let it get me down.

He *possibly* didn't remember what he'd said.

Not likely since he'd already told me, *Drunk dicking. Ten out of ten would recommend* so I figured he had a pretty good idea what he'd said.

Did he regret saying it?

Fear I would be mad?

Not really mean it?

Either way, I had things I wanted to say—*needed* to say— and I'd be saying them before we signed that contract of sale. Whether he felt the same or not, I couldn't go on without being honest and without knowing how he felt.

Plus, depending on how things with us worked out, there was possibly a lot of really sucky conversations in our future about what to do with Piping Hot after the divorce. I'd never fight him for the shop—it was his dream and I'd never take it from him. But the thought of our little business no longer being *ours* was killer and it would be best to get that shit out of the way if Justin didn't want what I wanted.

I think I love you and I don't want this thing to come to an end.

His words echoed over and over in my head.

I didn't know what it meant that he wasn't willing to say them or even discuss them in the light of a sober morning, but I did know I was going to cling tightly to them as we worked our way toward final signing day.

"Can you believe it's been a year already?" Justin said as he flitted around the kitchen. He was nervous about the signing the next day, but he seemed extra anxious about something.

I couldn't blame him because I was also a bundle of nerves.

We'd finished dinner and I had every intention of sitting him down and spilling my guts about my feelings and what I hoped could happen between us.

"In some ways, it seems like forever has passed," I said. "In other moments, it seems like it was just yesterday we got into this crazy adventure." That much was true. I waved a bottle of wine and raised my brow.

"Oh God, no," Justin said with a shiver. "Seriously, it may be this time next year before I can drink wine again. Just the thought has me reliving that nightmare hangover—who has a hangover for two days?"

I laughed. "Coffee? Tea?"

Justin rubbed his hands on his lounge pants. "Um, tea. Wanna watch TV?"

"Are you going to be able to sleep a wink tonight?"

"Huh?"

"You seem really nervous." I set the water to boil before taking him in my arms. "The paperwork was all fair and binding, I don't think Jo will have any surprises for us like last time."

Justin leaned into me. "Oh, uh, yeah. She really threw us for a loop with that. No, I trust things to go as planned. Just excited I guess."

When we had our tea mugs in hand, we made our way to the living room and settled on the couch.

I'd told myself I'd know when the time was right to spill my guts, but I was definitely second-guessing everything at that moment.

Maybe it was bad timing.

Maybe telling Justin I was in love with him and wanted us to stay married would be too much on the eve of our big day.

Maybe he'd tell me he didn't feel the same and I'd be ruined for the signing.

Maybe you should stop overthinking things and just talk to him.

Right.

I'd been tiptoeing around the truth for far too long. At nearly half a century old, I had no excuse for not speaking my mind and taking control of a situation.

Without turning on the television, I took Justin's hand and played through the words I'd been reciting in my head for weeks.

He clung to my hand like a drowning man and took a deep shuddering breath before turning my way.

"I'm sorry," he blurted.

"About what?" I asked in surprise.

Justin shook his head. "I've got a shit-ton to say, just let me word vomit myself all over before asking questions, yeah?"

My brows furrowed but I nodded.

"I'm sorry for telling you I loved you when I was drunk," Justin said.

My stomach plummeted.

"And I'm sorry for not wanting to talk about it the next morning. I *knew* talking about it would have been the best thing—the *mature* thing—but I was so damn worried you'd tell me you didn't feel the same. It was easier to bury my head and pretend everything was okay despite our time ticking down."

I opened my mouth to protest, but Justin shot me a look. I shut my mouth. What was he saying? Was he sorry for telling me he loved me or worried I wouldn't feel the same?

"I don't know if I've been lying to myself, lying to you, or a generous helping of both, but I've never been okay with knowing this was going to end," Justin continued. "In the *very* beginning, sure, I figured six months and say goodbye. No harm, no foul. But even before we knew this had to be for a year, I was already dreading the split." He held my hand, caressing his thumb over mine. "I don't know how it happened—grabbing a stranger's hand in the middle of a coffee shop, proclaiming you're engaged, and then getting married in order to buy a business hardly ever works out…or at least I'd think it hardly ever works out, it's not like I've done it multiple times—but somehow, you and I just clicked." Justin shot a nervous glance my way before he went back to studying my hand. "Maybe it was because we went into it knowing there was an end and it wasn't real, but it quickly became real to me. I've never been involved with someone like you and this has been the easiest relationship of my entire life."

Justin took a deep breath. "So, what I said when I was drunk was true, but I owe you more than a drunken confession." He squeezed my hand. "I've been really good with rule number one except for one thing and I'm sorry for that. Morgan, I love you and I don't want this thing between us to end after the sale." He bit his lip and winced. "I know it's a lot to throw at you and I'll understand if you don't…"

I yanked him toward me and kissed him, long and hard, as his words washed over me. Breaking from the kiss, I brushed my thumb over his bottom lip. "Open and honest, right? I love you."

Justin's eyes went wide. "For real?"

"How could I not?" I cupped his cheek. "The day you grabbed my hand and announced we were getting married was the day my life started again. Moving to Briarton, meeting Harley and Jo Ellen, working at the coffee shop, those were all things I needed to do to move on, but there'd been something missing." Leaning in, I pressed a kiss to his lips. "That missing piece was you. You gave me something to focus on, something to be excited about, a purpose. And as easy as it was to fall into being your friend and business partner, it was even easier to fall in love with you. I let myself start imagining we could make this thing work, that it didn't have to end—I didn't *want* it to end."

"Why didn't you tell me?" Justin whispered.

"Doubt and fear." I shrugged. "I didn't want to let myself hope someone as great as you would want to spend your life with me. There's so much between us that shouldn't even work—our age being something that *will* be an issue when I'm old and frail and you're still in peak condition, but selfishly, I love you so damn much I'm willing to push that worry aside for now. As the date of the final sale got closer and closer, I realized I was nearly fifty years old and I had to speak my truth, whether you wanted to hear it or not." Kissing him again, I went on. "You just beat me to it. Why didn't *you* tell me?"

Justin nibbled on his lip. "Same as you, I guess. Fear and doubt. I also felt guilty—I'd dragged you into this crazy scheme that turned into more than we'd planned, I didn't feel right dropping all these feelings on you. Maybe you'd been counting down the days to your escape. Maybe you couldn't wait to be rid of me. But then I realized I didn't want to become some cliché where lack of communication leads to regret and heartache—yeah, I sucked at some parts of rule number one, but I decided I couldn't let things end without a fight."

I pulled him into my arms and held him tight. "I love you," I murmured against his neck. "I'm sorry we were both idiots this whole time."

Justin nuzzled his nose against the sensitive skin under my ear. "So, we're doing this? Signing off on the final sale and staying married?"

I nodded. "That's what I want. Unless you'd rather go back to the beginning and date? We can work our way up to being married."

He scowled. "We've been married a year, living together, sleeping together, and having out-of-this-world sex, not to mention working together daily. I'm pretty sure we're way past the *dating* portion of this whole situation." He cuddled into my chest. "But I'm not going to turn down date night from time-to-time."

I smiled and pressed a kiss to the top of his head. "Date night is a must, I agree. And weekends away. And we have to keep up with rule number one."

"I'm pretty sure rule number two is also a must."

I cocked my head to the side and tried to remember the other rules. "Monogamy? Yeah, let's keep that one."

Wincing, Justin asked, "Rule number three is the kicker. What about *tell no one*? Do we keep this whole debacle to ourselves and let Harley and Jo continue on, none-the-wiser? Or do we tell them the truth?"

Rubbing a hand up and down his back, I huffed. "If we refer back to rule number one, we likely need to tell them. We could probably keep it to ourselves, but it kinda seems like bad karma to go into this relationship for real knowing we've been lying to them the whole time."

"How mad do you think they'll be?"

I shrugged. "I'm guessing we'll get something along the lines of *not mad, just disappointed*."

"Ouch. Well, I say we clear the air with them tomorrow so we can go into our new year of marriage with no secrets."

I stood from the couch and pulled Justin up, wrapping him in my arms and kissing him deeply. "Would my no-longer-fake-or-temporary-husband like to move things to the bedroom?"

Justin quickly resumed kissing me, licking into my mouth, making me moan. "Mmm, yes, please."

By the time we tumbled onto the bed, we'd stripped from our clothes, leaving a trail of pants, shirts, socks, and underwear behind us. I reached for the lube, tossing it onto the mattress as we writhed and rolled, our bodies connected from lips to toes.

"What do you want?" I asked, panting against Justin's ear as he rocked his hips against mine.

"You. Inside me." He stroked my cock. "Now."

Justin grabbed the lube and slicked his fingers before reaching behind him and pressing two digits into his hole as he gasped. As he worked himself open, he straddled my waist before reaching for my dick and smearing it with lube. Positioning my cock against his tight hole, Justin inched his way down my shaft with tiny grunts and whimpers as he adjusted to my invasion.

When Justin leaned forward and gripped the headboard, I grabbed his hips and held tight. He rode me slowly, taking my dick deep as he stared down at me. "Oh fuck," he panted, "so damn good." As he shifted and rose up slightly, Justin increased his speed for a few moments before pausing. "Fuck me," he demanded. "Hard and fast."

Not needing to be told twice, I dug my fingers into his hips and pistoned my hips, loving the way his tight channel opened for me and clung to my thrusting cock.

Each pounding thrust drove a whimper from Justin as his pre-cum leaked and dripped onto my stomach. "Jack yourself. Wanna see you come on me with my cock in your ass."

Justin took his dick in hand and began to stroke in time to my thrusts, his ass slamming down on me each time I rocked my hips upward. "Fuck, fuck," he grunted, "I'm gonna come. Fuck." He shuddered, his ass clenching around me as long, hot, creamy ropes shot onto my abdomen.

The heat and friction of his body gripping mine was too much and I lost myself to my orgasm, pulsing my release deep.

Wincing as he shifted off me, my spent dick slapping against my stomach, Justin reached for a towel and cleaned us up the best he could before snuggling into my arms. "Wanna do that again, but need sleep. Shower after round two." Pressing a kiss against my chest, he whispered, "Love you."

Brushing my lips against his temple, I couldn't help the warmth that coursed through me and the smile filling my face. "Love you, too."

When I woke later, I noticed the glow of the clock telling me we'd been asleep a couple hours. Justin groaned behind me, pressing his hard cock into the cleft of my ass.

"Got something in mind?" I teased.

"Thought I'd put my tools and natural ability to good use." His gruff words rumbled against my neck.

"Doing what?"

"Fucking you into the mattress," Justin growled.

Without another word, I rolled to my stomach as Justin flipped open the lid on the lube bottle. When his fingers slicked my hole, I spread my legs and gripped the sheets in anticipation.

Justin positioned himself on top of me and pressed his blunt head to my entrance. As he worked himself in inch-by-inch, I breathed through the burning stretch and welcomed his thick intrusion.

When his balls connected with my skin, Justin lowered his entire body to cover mine. His heaving chest pressed against my back as he whispered at my ear, "You okay?"

"Mmhm. Better when you move," I said, turning my head and offering him my lips.

Justin devoured my mouth as he began to rock his hips into me. Moments later, as I spread my legs farther apart, he continued his deep thrusts and added a grinding motion that set my blood to boiling.

"You feel so fucking amazing," Justin murmured against my ear. "Gonna come."

"Do it," I gasped. "Come in me." The friction of my throbbing cock against the bed and Justin's dick grazing that sweet spot deep inside was more than enough to send me over the edge. I groaned my release, loving the way my muscles tightened around Justin's slick, pulsing cock as he unloaded inside me.

Justin rested on my back for several moments as we both caught our breaths.

By the time we dragged ourselves to the shower, I knew we *had* to get some actual sleep or we'd be zombies at the contract signing.

And we definitely needed our wits about us when we told Jo Ellen and Harley we'd been faking it for a year.

SEVENTEEN

JUSTIN

THE SIGNING WENT off without a hitch and Morgan gripped my hand tightly when we were officially the sole owners of Piping Hot. Or maybe he was gripping my hand because he was as nervous as I was about telling Jo and Harley about our deception.

"Um, we wanted to talk to you about something," I said after clearing my throat.

Jo raised a brow and Harley sipped his coffee.

"So, back when we all first met, I mistakenly thought Morgan was the shop owner and spilled my guts to him before Jo Ellen walked in," I explained. "Once I heard you were only willing to sell to people who met the *family-owned* feel you were looking for, I pounced on Morgan and announced we were engaged."

Jo seemed to be fighting a smile and Harley just watched me over his mug.

"Well, it was all fake," I rushed on. "Morgan and I had just met moments before. We agreed to get married with the plan of just divorcing about six months in. This all started as a complete farce and we're sorry for lying to you."

"We know," Harley said.

My grandpa's words caught me off guard. "Wait, what? You know?"

"We know it was fake and we know you're sorry," Jo Ellen said calmly. "I guess our only question now is, are you still lying to yourselves that there's nothing between you or are you ready to admit you're in love with each other?"

Morgan snorted and I gaped.

"Wait, you knew? This whole time, you knew?" I sputtered.

"We had a pretty good feeling," Harley said with a grin. "You two aren't very good liars, but I will say, it got easier and easier to believe as time went on."

Jo leaned forward, elbows on the table. "So, what's the status now? Am I going to be pissed off that my favorite couple gets divorced and messes up my *family-owned* theme? Or did it all work out the way I hoped and you've figured out you're better together than following through with the ridiculous plan to go your separate ways?"

Morgan chuckled. "I can't believe you knew."

"We weren't born yesterday," Jo deadpanned. "We could have been wrong, but the look of surprise on Morgan's face and the desperation in Justin's words that first day were enough to make us suspicious. Honestly, we almost called you on it way back then, but opted to see how it would play out. We've just been wondering if you could actually pull it off and how long it would be before you broke down and told the truth."

I huffed. "Well, you'll be happy to know we've pulled our heads from our asses and realized we love each other. We have no intention of divorcing."

Jo clapped her hands and Harley smiled.

"And you'll let us plan a renewal of vows and *real*

reception?" Jo phrased it as a question, but it was clear she wasn't giving us an option of saying no.

I glanced toward Morgan and he nodded so I shrugged. "Sure. Plan away." I took Morgan's hand. "I'm good with doing it again for real."

My heart soared when he nodded and gave my hand a squeeze.

We stood in Harley's backyard with a yard full of friends and family just over a year from the day we first married. The officiant smiled and welcomed everyone to our vow renewal before speaking of the love, devotion, support, and dedication needed to make a marriage work.

"Did you want to exchange rings this time around?" the man asked.

Morgan cleared his throat and pulled my original ring from his pocket. "Something Justin doesn't know about this ring is the reason behind why I bought it over a year ago. During my first marriage, my husband wasn't keen on wearing a wedding band. Not because he didn't love me wholeheartedly, jewelry just wasn't his style and he wanted to avoid questions at work." He squeezed my hand as his words gripped my heart. "I wasn't hurt by this, but I did often long for that moment when I slipped a ring on the hand of the man I loved. When Justin and I did this the first time around, I knew it was meant to be temporary," he paused as the townsfolk chuckled; most had heard of our farce of a marriage because nothing stays secret for long in a small town, "but I selfishly wanted that moment when I saw *my* ring slide onto a man's finger. At the time, I knew it was ridiculous to think a ring on Justin's finger meant anything real—it was basically just a prop—but as time went on and I fell deeper and deeper in love with him, knowing he wore my ring started to mean something more to me." Morgan took my hand as I fought back tears. "Justin, I know we had the option of buying new, fancier rings, but I love that we kept these. Every day, every time you look at this simple metal band, I want you to remember where we started and how far we've come together. I want this ring to remind you I will always rub your feet and make you take breaks. I'll stay sober when you need to drink bottles of wine—yes, I said *bottles*," Morgan said to the gathered crowd with a wink, "and I will forever sample your amazing baking." He slid the ring over my finger, holding it in place as he continued, "I will always honor rule number one and you can count on me to tie your ties from here until the end of time." Morgan's words caught in his throat and he swallowed with a smile as he blinked away tears. "I love you and vow to spend the rest of my life showing you how much."

Murmurs and gushing erupted through the crowd as the officiant looked at me. "Do you have vows?"

I reached into my pocket and chuckled. "I should have gone first," I grumbled and the crowd laughed. "Morgan, I will forever be grateful for that crazy day when you accepted my ludicrous idea and helped me make my dream come true. Selfishly, I wish I could have done more for you, but thank you for supporting me, sticking by my side, and traveling this crazy adventure with me…"

Morgan held a finger to my lips. "As the elder here, I'm going to interrupt for just a moment."

I widened my eyes and smiled. "You're cutting me off mid-vow?"

He smiled broadly, "Only because it's important. Now, respect your elders," he said with a wink. "Before you go any further, I need you to get it through your thick head—maybe you've been exposed to too many sugar fumes or caffeine—

but *this* crazy life with you *is* my dream. Our business, the town, falling in love, our partnership, all of that is a dream I never thought I deserved or needed—not a dream I ever thought I'd get—but one I longed for all the same." He cupped my face. "Don't you *ever* think you aren't responsible for giving me my dream."

I cleared my throat and dashed a tear from my eyes. "Well, now that I've been upstaged—*twice*—I'll just go ahead and finish." I waited for the chuckles to die down. "Morgan, I love you more than I ever thought I could love anyone. I vow to honor rule number one, go on runs with you, allow you to rub my feet, and keep you in baked goods until death do us part. I'll forever need you to tie my ties, take me away when I need a break, and be my sounding board for business ideas. You are the piece of my life puzzle I didn't know was missing and I'll spend the rest of my life loving you." I slipped the ring onto Morgan's finger, the story he'd told of *why* he'd bought our rings last year still causing my heart to flutter.

After a few more words from the officiant, we were reintroduced as Mr. and Mr. Wade-Perry and the reception began almost immediately. Our first choice in DJ, Alex Goode, was booked at least a year out, so Jo had settled for a guy from a neighboring town. Our original photographer hadn't been able to come back from college for the event, so we'd asked guests to snap pictures and upload them to a Google Drive or tag us on social media.

I'd made all of the baked goods and Piping Hot had supplied the drinks. Thanks to Wayne's Grocery, we had a wide spread of food for our guests.

"Thank you all for coming," Jo Ellen's voice crackled from the speakers as everyone mingled. "Before our guests-of-honor share their first dance *again*, I had a little story I wanted to tell."

I frowned through my smile as Harley took his place next to Jo.

"A little over a year ago—and by now, most of you know this story—these two knuckleheads thought they could pull one over on me by faking a marriage and buying my coffee shop." Jo Ellen gave us a wink. "Well, the moment I had an inkling of what was going on, I started conspiring. After all, if they could have a secret and try to deceive, so could I. When it was time to sell the shop, I convinced them they had to go through a trial period of a year before I'd be willing to sell it free and clear." Jo shrugged. "I figured a year would be enough time to convince them they were perfect for each other and show them they didn't need to go their separate ways after they owned Piping Hot for real."

My mouth dropped open and Morgan snorted next to me.

"What can I say?" Jo shrugged and leaned into Harley as his arm went around her. "This kooky old woman is a romantic at heart and I had every hope these two would eventually work it out."

"What are you saying?" I asked, thinking I was pretty sure, but wanting confirmation.

"I'm saying you two have officially owned Piping Hot since last year. I simply created the story of needing a year-long trial period in hopes of keeping you together," Jo said with a big smile. "Luckily, you didn't question it or ask your own attorney to check out the paperwork."

"You sneaky thing," Morgan said as he laughed before kissing the top of my head.

Jo and Harley shrugged. "You aren't the only ones who can keep secrets," Harley said proudly. "We're glad it all worked out—the shop *and* the marriage."

"Well, without further ado, and in celebration of both the vows *and* the business, let's let these two dance to their song," Jo said. "Which, by the way, will forever remain one of the tell-tale signs that clued me in to your scheme. But it all worked out and you two completely deserve to be *stuck* with each other."

Morgan grabbed my hand as the music started. "Guess I really am *stuck with you* now, huh?"

"You had a year to decide you wanted out. It's too late now. You love me and there are no takebacks," I whispered against his ear.

He laughed, the deep rumble sending warm vibrations through my body. "No one else I'd rather be stuck with. Definitely no takebacks."

EPILOGUE

MORGAN

One Year Later

"You know, this song really is good for us," Justin said as he hummed along to "Stuck with You" while I spun him around the deck as our song played.

"How so?" I asked, nuzzling his cheek.

"Just listen to the lyrics. *You never let me down. I could stay here a lifetime. Can't fight this no more, it's just you and me. There's nowhere we need to be. Kinda hope we're here forever.*" He shrugged as he repeated random lyrics from the song. "I know it wasn't written to be a wedding song and it wasn't *actually* our song when I blurted it out, but I think it works well." He grunted as I dipped him. "Plus, we'll always have a story to tell."

We'd had a huge two-year celebration—of our marriage and the shop—a couple days earlier. Justin had kicked ass with mini Bundt cakes and cake cups for our guests. Each customer got Piping Hot mugs with already-half-filled loyalty cards tied to a ribbon. The day had been perfect, but we'd wanted our actual anniversary to be just for us.

"Are you ready for your gifts?" Justin asked.

"Gifts? Plural? I only got you one thing," I said, but I knew it wouldn't matter.

Justin shrugged. "Eh, no biggie. You can just give me a good dicking tonight and we'll call it even."

I threw my head back and laughed. "You're too easy."

"Sit down."

I sat on the deck bench.

"Remember way back when we started having sex and we were discussing strenuous activities?"

I frowned, but nodded.

"Well, part of your anniversary present is I signed us up for a half-marathon. I figure our strenuous activities can now include sex *and* ridiculously long runs."

My mouth dropped open. "For real?"

He beamed. "Yep, it's in six months. I figure that's enough time for us to slowly up our distance so I don't die."

I stood and wrapped him in my arms. "Thank you. I love this gift."

"Well, the second part is as much for me as it for you. It's supposed to be here tomorrow." He handed me a paper with an infrared sauna pictured.

"You got me a sauna?" I gaped.

"No, I got *us* a sauna. There's no way I can run thirteen point one miles without needing the services of the hot tub, a sauna, *and* your dick."

I laughed. "This is possibly the best anniversary ever. Thank you."

Justin kissed me. "Okay, I'm ready for my gift. Not the dicking, that's for later."

Chuckling, I pulled up the photo app on my phone and swiped to the correct picture. I handed the phone to Justin.

"Aww, the cabin. Are you taking me there again?"

"Yes," I said as I took the phone from him. "But it's a bit different this time. With all the work we've been doing at

Piping Hot and how busy we'll be getting our second shop set up, we're going to *need* a place to get away." We were breaking ground on another Piping Hot a couple towns over very soon. "So, instead of constantly renting the cabin," I paused and bit my lip, "I bought it."

"You what?" Justin's eyes bugged. "The cabin is ours? The whole thing? Completely ours? Not like a time-share?"

"One hundred percent ours and I demand we spend enough time there to get our money's worth," I murmured against his mouth as I kissed him.

Justin pulled back. "We will, I promise. I'm in love with that cabin." He scowled and got a far-off look in his eyes. "Ohhhh, what if we plan ahead for the times we want to stay there and the other times we rent it out? It could be a great source of income." He slapped me against the chest. "*And* we'll stock it for our guests with Piping Hot coffees and teas along with baked goods—it's an amazing advertising opportunity."

Staring at my husband in wonder, I could only laugh and kiss him again. "Have I ever told you how much I love you and your amazing mind?"

"Yeah," Justin quipped, "but I'll never get tired of it."

"Tomorrow, let's map out some plans. But today…"

"Today we have a picnic lunch and tonight is for the dicking," Justin finished for me as he reached for the blanket and picnic basket.

I swatted at his ass as we headed to the yard and settled between a young oak tree and our garden. Justin spread the blanket and I opened the basket. Once the food and wine were out, we began to eat and Justin waved a hand toward the tree.

"James would be super proud of you, I think," he said.

As we both studied the oak we'd planted in memory of James—with his ashes spread on the roots—I smiled. "Yeah, I think he would be." We'd chosen the oak as a symbol of strength and longevity and planted it as a tribute to James. We planned to be in Briarton for years to come, so having a piece of James there with me meant a lot. "He'd be proud of you, too. He was a businessman at heart and he would have loved the way your mind works."

"Happy anniversary," Justin whispered as we clinked glasses. "I will forever be grateful for whatever god of fate brought you to Briarton and into my life. I love you."

"Happy two years," I said. "Thank you for pulling me into your crazy scheme and giving me a reason to breathe again. I love you."

I knew we'd had an unconventional start and there'd be bumps along the way, but my life once again had meaning and I looked forward to an amazing future with Justin as we navigated our life together.

He took my wine glass and cupped my face in his hand. "Now, I know the actual dicking down is later, but how do you feel about a little preview of tonight right now?"

I laughed as Justin yanked me to standing and pulled me toward the door.

"Our picnic," I protested.

"The ants can have it. We have more important things to do," Justin promised as he took off sprinting toward the bedroom. "Gotta work on increasing my stamina if I'm going to be ready for the half-marathon."

Tackling him to the mattress, I caught his lips in mine and kissed him deeply. "Then by all means, let the training begin."

~The End~

Want more of Briarton? Grab Perfect Timing now!

ALSO BY A.D. ELLIS

Perfect Timing is a steamy, M/M romance with an introverted, demisexual writer and a big, soft teddy bear of a nurse trying to navigate a love they've always dreamed of but most definitely weren't expecting.

Adore (Remington Place 1) is a steamy, age-gap, bi-awakening, dad's best friend M/M romance with a sassy smartass and a sexy silver fox. It's the first book in the Remington Place series and can be read as a stand-alone.

Crave (Remington Place 2) is a steamy, friends-to-lovers, fake relationship M/M romance with a virgin nursing student and a gruff, grumbly construction worker.

Desire (Remington Place 3) is a steamy, age-gap, hurt/comfort M/M romance featuring a heart-of-gold mechanic and a twink who's a lot stronger than he realizes. *Please note: This story has mention of sex trafficking and sexual abuse.*

Yearn (Remington Place 4)- a steamy, enemies-to-lovers, forced proximity M/M romance between two EMS workers who have hated each other for a decade.

Power Struggle is a steamy M/M, age-gap, forced proximity romance set in a small town. A twenty-year history, rival schools and jobs, and a hotel with only one bed make for a hot and heavy, sweet and sexy, HEA-guaranteed love story.

Take Me Home M/M age-gap, opposites-attract romance with plenty of steam and a scene that will make you appreciate camouflage and work boots

Let Love In M/M age-gap, forced proximity, dad's best friend, bisexual-awakening romance. Available on AUDIO!

Let Love Win M/M brother's best friend romance. Available on AUDIO!

Buried Secrets Romantic suspense stand-alone title. Available on AUDIO!

Silver in the City (3 books- meet the Silver crew you read about in Forged in the City) Available on AUDIO!

Forged in the City (3 books- a spin-off series from Silver in the City) Available on AUDIO

The BJ Boys Series (3 books, small town, big love) Available on AUDIO

Forever Better Together (friends to lovers) Available on AUDIO!

His Reluctant Cowboy (age gap, opposites attract, cowboy romance) Available on AUDIO!

What Blooms Beneath (LGBT Fantasy romance) Available on AUDIO!

Sawyer

(this was the first M/M I wrote and you may remember Sawyer and Luke being mentioned in Barrett & Ivan as well as in Ryker & Gavin)

Start Something About Him with a **FREE** short story:

(The Beginning https://instafreebie.com/free/84Cxr)

Then continue with the other stand-alone titles in the series (available to read FREE for Kindle Unlimited subscribers):

Bryan & Jase

Brody & Nick

Barrett & Ivan

Braeton & Drew

Ryker & Gavin

Kade & Cameron

Or grab the boxset HERE.

Plus several other titles:

Devoted (a Something About Him novella)

Saving Us

Stranded Hearts (a short story)

Eli & Gage (a Something About Him short story)

Escape (a 3-book collection of fun stories)

A.D.'s first stories (all male/female except <u>Sawyer</u> which is male/male) are in the Torey Hope and Torey Hope: The Later Years series. Find the 8 book box set HERE or you can find each individual title on Amazon.

For Nicky

Because of Beckett

Christmas in Torey Hope

Loving Josie

Decker

Sawyer

Zach

Kendrick

ACKNOWLEDGMENTS

It's always so hard to write this part because I'm worried I'll forget someone without meaning to.

Readers- you are the reason I write. As long as you continue reading my stories, I'll continue writing them. Thank you for your support.

Bloggers- your support, reviews, and promotion are very much appreciated. Thank you!

My author buddies- I don't know that I could keep doing this without our brainstorm sessions, laughter, road trips, meals, wine, and friendship as my support.

Thank you to my alpha readers, betas, editors, proofreaders, and ARC readers! Your eyes and input are beyond important to me.

Brett and Gage- as usual, I doubt you even grasp how much your support, input, and friendship mean to me. This author journey has brought many wonderful things into my life, and you both are two of the BEST! I'm blessed to call you friends.

My family and friends- thank you for your love and support, always.

ABOUT THE AUTHOR

A.D. Ellis is an Indiana girl, born and raised. She spends much of her time in central Indiana as a teacher in the inner city of Indianapolis, being a mom to two amazing teens, and wondering how she and her husband of over two decades have managed to not drive each other insane. A lot of her time is also devoted to phone call avoidance and her hatred of cooking.

She loves chocolate, wine, pizza, and naps along with reading and writing romance. These loves don't leave much time for housework, much to the chagrin of her husband. Who would pick cleaning the house over a nap or a good book? She uses any extra time to increase her fluency in sarcasm.

Sign up at http://www.subscribepage.com/ADEllisNewsMMRomance for a FREE male/male romance book.

Find all of my books at Amazon- https://www.amazon.com/A.D.-Ellis/e/B00K0YJ8CW

Follow my website http://www.adellisauthor.com or find me on Facebook

http://www.facebook.com/adellisauthor

Check out my TikTok- https://www.tiktok.com/@adellisauthor

You can also find me on Twitter http://www.twitter.com/ADEllisAuthor